PULP

Other Charles Bukowski novels available from Virgin Books:

Post Office
Factotum
Women

PULP

Charles Bukowski

Dedicated to bad writing

This edition first published in 2004 by
Virgin Books Ltd
Thames Wharf Studios
Rainville Road
London
W6 9HA

A catalogue record for this book is available from the
British Library.

ISBN 1 85227 200 7

Typeset by TW Typesetting, Plymouth, Devon
Printed and bound in Great Britain by Mackays of Chatham

1

I was sitting in my office, my lease had expired and McKelvey was starting eviction proceedings. It was a hellish hot day and the air conditioner was broken. A fly crawled across the top of my desk. I reached out with the open palm of my hand and sent him out of the game. I wiped my hand on my right pants leg as the phone rang.

I picked it up. 'Ah yes,' I said.

'Do you read Celine?' a female voice asked. Her voice sounded quite sexy. I had been lonely for some time. Decades.

'Celine,' I said, 'ummm . . .'

'I want Celine,' she said. 'I've got to have him.'

Such a sexy voice, it was getting to me, really.

'Celine?' I said. 'Give me a little background. Talk to me, lady. Keep talking . . .'

'Zip up,' she said.

I looked down.

'How did you know?' I asked.

'Never mind. I want Celine.'

'Celine is dead.'

'He isn't. I want you to find him. I want him.'

'I might find his bones.'

'No, you fool, he's alive!'

'Where?'

'Hollywood. I hear he's been hanging around Red Koldowsky's bookstore.'

'Then why don't *you* find him?'

'Because first I want to know if he's the *real* Celine. I have to be sure, quite sure.'

'But why did you come to me? There are a hundred dicks in this town.'

'John Barton recommended you.'

'Oh, Barton, yeah. Well, listen, I'll have to have some kind of advance. And I'll have to see you personally.'

'I'll be there in a few minutes,' she said.

She hung up. I zipped up.

And waited.

2

She walked in.

Now, I mean, it just wasn't fair. Her dress fit so tight it almost split the seams. Too many chocolate malts. And she walked on heels so high they looked like little stilts. She walked like a drunken cripple, staggering around the room. A glorious dizziness of flesh.

'Sit down, lady,' I said.

She put it down and crossed her legs high, damn near knocked my eyes out.

'It's good to see you, lady,' I said.

'Stop gawking, please. It's nothing that you haven't seen before.'

'You're wrong there, lady. Now may I have your name?'

'Lady Death.'

'Lady Death? You from the circus? The movies?'

'No.'

'Place of birth?'

'It doesn't matter.'

'Year of birth?'

'Don't try to be funny . . .'

'Just trying to get some background . . .'

I got lost somehow, began staring up her legs. I was always a leg man. It was the first thing I saw when I was born. But then I was trying to get out. Ever since I have been working in the other direction and with pretty lousy luck.

She snapped her fingers.

'Hey, come out of it!'

'Huh?' I looked up.

'The Celine case. Remember?'

'Yeah, sure.'

I unfolded a paperclip, pointed the end toward her.

'I'll need a check for services rendered.'

'Of course,' she smiled. 'What are your rates?'

'6 dollars an hour.'

She got out her checkbook, scribbled away, ripped the check out and tossed it to me. It landed on the desk.

I picked it up. $240. I hadn't seen that much money since I hit an exacta at Hollywood Park in 1988.

'Thank you, Lady . . .'

'. . . Death,' she said.

'Yes,' I said. 'Now fill me in a little on this so-called Celine. You said something about a bookstore?'

'Well, he's been hanging around Red's bookstore, browsing . . . asking about Faulkner, Carson McCullers. Charles Manson . . .'

'Hangs around the bookstore, huh? Hmm . . .'

'Yes,' she said, 'you know Red. He likes to run people out of his bookstore. A person can spend a thousand bucks in there, then maybe linger a minute or two and Red will say, "Why don't you get the hell out of here?" Red's a good guy, he's just freaky. Anyway, he keeps tossing Celine out and Celine goes over to Musso's and hangs around the bar looking sad. A day or so later he'll be back and it will happen all over again.'

'Celine is dead. Celine and Hemingway died a day apart. 32 years ago.'

'I know about Hemingway. I got Hemingway.'

'You sure it was Hemingway?'

'Oh yeah.'

'Then how come you can't be sure this Celine is the real Celine?'

'I don't know. I've got some kind of block with this thing. It's never happened before. Maybe I've been in the game too long. So, I've come to you. Barton says you're good.'

'And you think the real Celine is alive? You want him?'

'Real bad, buster.'

4

'Belane. Nick Belane.'

'All right, Belane. I want to make *sure*. It's got to be the *real* Celine, not just some half-assed wannabe. There are too many of those.'

'Don't we know it.'

'Well, get on it. I want France's greatest writer. I've waited a long time.'

Then she got up and walked out of there. I never saw an ass like that in my life. Beyond concept. Beyond everything. Don't bother me now. I want to think about it.

3

It was the next day.

I had cancelled my appointment to speak before the Palm Springs Chamber of Commerce.

It was raining. The ceiling leaked. The rain dripped down through the ceiling and went 'spat, spat, spat, a spat a spat, spat, spat, spat, a spat, spat, spat, a spat, a spat, a spat, spat, spat, spat . . .'

The *sake* kept me warm. But a warm what? A warm zero. Here I was 55 years old and I didn't have a pot to catch rain in. My father had warned me that I would end up diddling myself on some stranger's back porch in Arkansas. And I still had time to make it. The Greyhounds ran every day. But busses constipated me and there was always some old Union Jack with a rancid beard who snored. Maybe it would be better to work on the Celine Case.

Was Celine Celine or was he somebody else? Sometimes I felt that I didn't even know who *I* was. All right, I'm Nicky Belane. But check this. Somebody could yell out, 'Hey, Harry! Harry Martel!' and I'd most likely answer, 'Yeah, what is it?' I mean, I could be anybody, what does it matter? What's in a name?

Life's strange, isn't it? They always chose me last on the baseball team because they knew I could drive that son-of-a-bitch out there, all the way to Denver. Jealous chipmunks, that's what they were!

I was gifted, am gifted. Sometimes I looked at my hands and realized that I could have been a great pianist or something. But what have my hands done? Scratched my balls, written checks, tied shoes, pushed toilet levers, etc. I have wasted my hands. And my mind.

I sat in the rain.

The phone rang. I wiped it dry with a past due bill from the IRS, picked it up.

'Nick Belane,' I said. Or was I Harry Martel?

'This is John Barton,' came the voice.

'Yes, you've been recommending me, thank you.'

'I've been watching you. You've got talent. It's a little raw but that's part of the charm.'

'Great to hear. Business has been bad.'

'I've been watching you. You'll make it, you just have to endure.'

'Yeah. Now, what can I do for you, Mr. Barton?'

'I am trying to locate the Red Sparrow.'

'The Red Sparrow? What the hell is that?'

6

'I'm sure it exists, I just want to find it, I want you to locate it for me.'

'Any leads for me to go on?'

'No, but I'm sure the Red Sparrow is out there somewhere.'

'This Sparrow doesn't have a name, does it?'

'What do you mean?'

'I mean, a name. Like Henry. Or Abner. Or Celine?'

'No, it's just the Red Sparrow and I know that you can find it. I've got faith in you.'

'This is going to cost you, Mr. Barton.'

'If you find the Red Sparrow I will give you one hundred dollars a month for life.'

'Hmm. . . . Listen, how about giving me all of it in a lump sum?'

'No, Nick, you'd blow it at the track.'

'All right, Mr. Barton, leave me your phone number and I'll work on it.'

Barton gave me the number, then said, 'I have real confidence in you, Belane.'

Then he hung up.

Well, business was picking up. But the ceiling was leaking worse than ever. I shook off some rain drops, had a hit of *sake*, rolled a cigarette, lit it, inhaled, then choked out a hacking cough. I put on my brown derby, turned on the telephone message machine, walked slowly toward the door, opened it and there stood McKelvey. He had a huge chest and looked like he was wearing shoulder pads.

'Your lease is up, punk!' he spit out. 'I want your dead ass out of here!'

Then I noticed his belly. It was like a soft mound of dead shit and I slammed my fist deep into it. His face doubled over into my upcoming knee. He fell, then rolled off to one side. Ghastly sight. I walked over, slipped out his wallet. Photos of children in pornographic poses.

I thought about killing him. But I just took his Gold Visa Card, kicked him in the ass and took the elevator down.

I decided to walk to Red's. When I drove I always seemed to get a parking ticket and the lots charged more than I could afford.

I walked toward Red's feeling a bit depressed. Man was born to die. What did it mean? Hanging around and waiting. Waiting for the 'A train.' Waiting for a pair of big breasts on some August night in a Vegas hotel room. Waiting for the mouse to sing. Waiting for the snake to grow wings. Hanging around.

Red was in.

'You're lucky,' he said, 'you just missed that drunk Chinaski. He was in here bragging about his new Pelouze postage scale.'

'Never mind that,' I said. 'You got a signed copy of Faulkner's *As I Lay Dying*?'

'Of course.'

'What's the toll?'

'2800 dollars.'

'I'll think about it . . .'

'Pardon me,' said Red.

Then he turned to a fellow thumbing through a first edition of *You Can't Go Home Again*.

'Please put that book in the case and get the hell out of here!'

It was a delicate-looking little fellow, all hunched over. Dressed in what looked like a yellow rubber suit.

He put the book back into the case and walked past us toward the street, his eyes clouding with moisture. And it had stopped raining. His yellow rubber suit was useless.

Red looked at me.

'Can you believe that some of them come in here eating icecream cones?'

'I believe worse than that.'

Then I noticed somebody else was in the bookstore. He was standing near the back. I thought I recognized him from his photos. Celine. Celine?

I walked slowly down toward him. I got real close. So close that I could see what he was reading. Thomas Mann. *The Magic Mountain*.

He saw me.

'This fellow has a problem,' he said, holding up the book.

'What's that?' I asked.

'He considers boredom an Art.'

He put the book back in the case and just stood there looking like Celine.

I looked at him.

'This is amazing,' I said.

'What is?' he asked.

'I thought that you were dead,' I told him.

He looked at me.

'I thought that you were dead too,' he said.

Then we just stood there looking at each other.

Then I heard Red.

'HEY, YOU!' he yelled, 'GET THE HELL OUT OF HERE!'

We were the only two in there.

'Which one to get the hell out?' I asked.

'THE ONE THAT LOOKS LIKE CELINE! GET THE HELL OUT OF HERE!'

'But why?' I asked.

'I CAN TELL WHEN THEY'RE NOT GOING TO BUY!'

Celine or whoever it was began to walk out. I followed him.

He walked up toward the boulevard, then stopped at the newsstand.

That newsstand had been there as long as I could remember. I recalled standing there two or three decades ago with 3 prostitutes. I took them all to my place and one of them masturbated my dog. They thought it was funny. They were drunk and on pills. Then one of the prostitutes went to the bathroom where she fell and banged her head against the edge of the toilet and bled all over the place. I kept wiping the stuff up with big wet towels. I put her to bed and sat with the others and finally they left. The one in bed stayed for 4 days and nights, drinking all my beer and talking about her two children in East Kansas City.

The fellow – was it Celine? – was standing at the newsstand reading a magazine. When I got closer I noticed that it was *The New Yorker*. He put it back in the rack and looked at me.

'Only one problem there,' he said.

'What's that?'

'They just don't know how to write. None of them.'

Just then, a cab came idling by.

'HEY, CABBY!' Celine yelled.

The cab slowed and he leaped forward, the back door opened and he was inside.

'HEY!' I yelled at him, 'I WANT TO ASK YOU SOMETHING!'

The cab was brisking toward Hollywood Boulevard. Celine leaned out, stuck out his arm, gave me the finger. Then he was gone.

First cab I had seen around those parts in decades. I mean, an empty one, just lolling by.

Well, the rain had stopped but the pain was still there. Also, there was now a chill in the air and everything smelled like wet farts.

I hunched over and moved toward Musso's.

I had the Gold Visa Card. I was alive. Maybe. I even began to feel like Nicky Belane. I hummed a little passage from Eric Coates.

Hell was what you made it.

4

I looked up Celine in the Webster. 1891–1961. It was 1993. Saying he was alive, that would make him 102 years old. No wonder Lady Death was looking for him.

And that fellow in the bookstore had looked between 40 and 50. So, that was it. He wasn't Celine. Or maybe he'd found a method to beat the aging process. Look at the movie stars, they took the skin from their ass and stuck it on the face. The skin on the ass was the last to wrinkle. They all walked around in their later years with buttock faces. Would Celine do that? Who would want to live to be 102? Nobody but a fool. Why would Celine wish to linger? The whole thing was crazy. Lady Death was crazy. I was crazy. The pilots of airliners were crazy. Never look at the pilot. Just get on board and order drinks.

I watched two flies fucking, then decided to call Lady Death. I unzipped and waited for her voice.

'Hello.' I heard her voice.

'Ummm . . .,' I said.

'What? Oh, it's you Belane. You getting anywhere on the case?'

'Celine is dead, he was born in 1891.'

'I'm aware of the statistics, Belane. Listen, I know that he is alive . . . somewhere . . . and the guy in the bookstore could be him. Are you closing in on anything? I want this guy. I want him badly.'

'Ummm . . .' I said.

'Zip up!'

'Huh?'

'You fool, I said, "zip up!" '

'Uh . . . all right . . .'

'I want positive proof whether this guy *is* or *isn't*! I've told you that I've got this crazy mind block on this matter. Barton recommended you, he said you were one of the best.'

'Oh yes, I'm also working for Barton right now, as a matter of fact. Trying to locate a Red Sparrow. What do you think about that?'

'Listen, Belane, you solve this Celine thing and I'll *tell* you where the Red Sparrow is.'

'Oh will you, Lady? Oh, I'd do anything for you!'

'Like what, Belane?'

'Well, I'd kill my pet cockroach for you, I'd belt-whip my mother if she was here, I'd . . .'

'Stop babbling! I'm beginning to think Barton may have given me a bum steer! Well, you better get going! Either solve this Celine thing or I'm coming after *you*!'

'Hey, wait a minute, Lady!'

The phone was dead in my hand. I placed it back in its cradle. Ow. She had no block of any sort in getting right to me.

I had work to do.

I looked around for a fly to kill.

Then the door swung open and there stood McKelvey and a big stack of subnormal manure. McKelvey looked at me, then nodded toward *it*.

'This is Tommy.'

Tommy looked at me with his tiny dim eyes.

'Pleased ta meatcha,' he said.

McKelvey grinned a horrible grin.

'Now, Belane, Tommy is here just for one purpose and that purpose is to slowly pound you to bloody henshit. Right, Tommy?'

'Uh huh,' said Tommy.

He looked like he weighed about 380. Well, shave his fur and you might get him down to 365.

I gave him a kindly smile.

'Now look, Tommy, you don't know me, do you?'

'Uh-uh.'

'Then why would you want to hurt me?'

'Because Mr. McKelvey told me to.'

'Tommy, if Mr. McKelvey told you to drink your peepee, would you do it?'

'Hey!' said McKelvey, 'stop mixing my boy up!'

'Tommy, would you eat your mother's poo-poo just because Mr. McKelvey told you to eat your mother's poo-poo?'

'Huh?'

'Shut up, Belane, I'll do the talking here!'

He turned to Tommy.

'Now, I want you to rip this guy apart like an old newspaper, just tear him to shreds and throw him to the fucking winds, got it?'

'I got it, Mr. McKelvey.'

'Good, then what are you waiting for, the last rose of summer?'

Tommy stepped toward me. I slipped the luger out of the drawer, pointed it towards Tommy's gross immensity.

'Hold it, Thomas, or you'll be spouting more red than the jerseys of the Stanford football team!'

'Hey,' said McKelvey, 'where'd you get that damned thing?'

'A dick without a gat is like a tomcat with a rubber. Or like a clock without hands.'

'Belane,' said McKelvey, 'you talk goofy.'

'I been told. Now tell your boy to back off or I'll put so much daylight through him that you'll be able to toss a grapefruit through!'

'Tommy,' said McKelvey, 'come on back here and stand in front of me.'

They stood there like that. I had to figure out what to do with them. It wasn't easy. I'd never won a scholarship to Oxford. I'd slept through biology and I was weak in math. But I had managed to stay alive up until now.

14

Maybe.

Anyhow, I momentarily held some kind of an ace in some kind of a stacked deck. I had to make a move. Now or never. September was coming. The crows were in council. The sun was bleeding.

'All right, Tommy,' I said, 'down on your hands and knees! Now!'

He looked at me like he didn't hear so good.

I gave him a wan smile and clicked the safety catch off the luger.

Tommy was dumb but not totally.

He dropped to his hands and knees, shaking the whole 6th floor like a 5.9 earthquake. My fake Dali fell to the floor. The one with the melted watch.

Tommy clumped there like the Grand Canyon and looked at me.

'Now, Tommy,' I said, 'you are going to be the elephant and McKelvey is going to be the elephant boy, got it?'

'Huh?' asked Tommy.

I looked over at McKelvey.

'Go on! Get on! Mount!'

'Belanc, are you nuts?'

'Who knows? Insanity is comparative. Who sets the norm?'

'I don't know,' said McKelvey.

'*Just get on!*'

'All right, all right! But I never had trouble like this before when a lease ran out.'

'Get on, *asshole!*'

McKelvey climbed onto Tommy's back. He had real trouble getting his legs over the sides. Almost split his butt.

'Good,' I said. 'Now, Tommy, you're the elephant and you're going to carry McKelvey on your back, down the hall and into the elevator. Begin now!'

Tommy began crawling across the floor of the office.

'Belane,' said McKelvey, 'I'll get you for this. I swear by my mother's pubic hairs!'

'Mess with me again, McKelvey, and I'll ram your cock down a garbage disposal!'

I opened the door and Tommy crawled out with the elephant boy.

He crawled on down the hall and as I slipped the luger back into my coat pocket I felt something in there, a crumpled up piece of paper. I took it out. It was my examination paper for the written test to renew my driver's license. It was full of red marks. I had failed.

I tossed the paper over my shoulder and followed my friends.

We reached the elevator and I pressed the button.

I stood there humming a bit from 'Carmen.'

Then out of nowhere I remembered long ago reading about how they found Jimmy Foxx dead in a skid row hotel room. All those home runs. Dead with the roaches.

The elevator came up. The door opened and I gave Tommy a boot in the ass. He crawled in bearing McKelvey. There were 3 people in there, standing, reading their newspapers.

They kept reading. The elevator went down.

I took the stairway. I was 30 pounds overweight. I needed it.

I counted 176 steps and then I was on the first floor. I stopped at the cigar stand, bought a cigar and *The Daily Racing Form*. I heard the elevator coming.

Outside, I moved through the smog resolutely. My eyes were blue and my shoes were old and nobody loved me. But I had things to do.

I was Nicky Belane, private detective.

5

Unfortunately, I ended up at the racetrack that afternoon and that night I got drunk. But the time wasn't wasted, I was cogitating, sifting out the facts. I was right on top of everything. Any moment, I'd have everything figured out. Sure.

6

The next day I took a chance and went back to the office. After all, what's a dick without an office?

I opened the door and who was sitting there behind my desk? Not Celine. Not the Red Sparrow. It was McKelvey. He gave me a sweet, false smile.

'Good morning, Belane, how they hanging?'

'Why do you ask? You want a peek?'

'No thanks.'

Then he scratched his, and yawned.

'Well, Nicky, my boy, your lease has been paid up for the next year by some mysterious benefactor.'

Lady Death, said a voice inside of my head, is playing with you.

'Anybody I know?' I asked.

'Swore on my mother's honor to keep it quiet.'

'Your mother's honor? She's handled more turkeyneck than the corner butcher!'

McKelvey rose up from behind the desk.

'Take it easy,' I told him, 'or I'll turn you into a basket case.'

'I don't like you getting on my mother.'

'Why not? Half the guys in this town have.'

McKelvey moved around the desk toward me.

'Come closer,' I said, 'and I'll have your head breathing up your butt.'

He stopped. I looked awesome when I was pissed.

'All right,' I said, 'fill me in. This benefactor . . . it was a woman, wasn't it?'

'Yeah. Yeah. Never saw a babe like that!'

His eyes looked glazed but they always looked like that.

'Come on, Mac, fill me in, tell me more . . .'

'I can't. I promised. Mother's honor.'

'Oh Christ,' I sighed. 'OK, get out of here, my lease is paid.'

McKelvey shuffled slowly toward the door. Then he looked back at me over his left shoulder.

'All right,' he said, 'but keep the place nice and clean. No parties, no crap games, no crap. You got a year.'

He walked to the door, opened it, closed it and was gone.

7

Well, I was back in my office.

Time to go to work. I picked up the phone and touchkeyed into my bookie.

'Tony's Pizza Take Out,' he answered, 'at your service.'

I gave him my code name.

'This is Mr. Slow Death.'

'Belane,' he said, 'you're into me for $475, I can't take your action. You've got to clean the slate first.'

'I've got a 25 buck bet, that will make half-a-string. If I lose I'll cough it all up, my mother's honor.'

'Belane, your mother is into me for $230.'

'Yeah? And your mother's got warts on her ass!'

'What? Listen, Belane, you been . . .?'

'No, no. It was another guy. He told me.'

'OK, then.'

'All right, I want $25 to win on *Burnt Butterfly* in the 6th.'

'All right, you're covered. And good luck. Yours seems to be running out.'

I hung up. Son-of-a-bitch, a man was born to struggle for each inch of ground. Born to struggle, born to die.

I thought about that. And thought about that.

Then I leaned back in my chair, took a good drag on my cigarette and blew an almost perfect smoke ring.

8

After lunch I decided to go back to the office. I opened the door and there was a guy sitting behind my desk. It wasn't McKelvey. I didn't know who it was. People liked to sit behind my desk. And, besides the guy sitting, there was a guy standing. They looked mean, calm but mean.

'My name's Dante,' said the guy behind the desk.

'And my name's Fante,' said the guy standing.

I didn't say anything. I was fumbling in the dark. A chill ran up my back and right on through the ceiling.

'Tony sent us,' said the guy sitting.

'Don't know a Tony. You gentlemen have the right address?'

'Oh yeah,' said the standing guy.

Then Dante said, '*Burnt Butterfly* ran out.'

'Tossed the jock coming out of the gate,' said Fante.

'You're kidding.'

'I'm not kidding. Ask the dust.'

'As a handicapper you are handicapped,' said Dante.

'And Tony says you owe us half-a-string,' said Fante.

'Oh that,' I said, 'I've got it right here . . .'

I moved toward my desk.

'Forget it, sucker,' Dante laughed. 'We've confiscated your water pistol.'

I stepped back.

'Now,' said Fante, 'you realize that we can't let you walk around blissfully sucking air while you owe Tony half-a-string?'

'Give me 3 days . . .'

'You got 3 minutes,' said Dante.

'Why is it?' I asked, 'that you guys take turns talking? First Dante, then Fante, on and on, don't you ever break your rhythm?'

'We're here to break something else,' they both spoke together. 'You.'

'That was good,' I said. 'I liked that. A duet.'

'Shut up,' said Dante. He pulled out a smoke and stuck it in his lips. 'Hmm,' he went on, 'seems like I forgot my lighter. Come here, asshole, light my cigarette.'

' "Asshole"? You talking to yourself?'

'No, *you*, asshole, come here. Light my smoke! Now!'

I found my lighter, walked forward, stopped in front of one of the ugliest faces I had ever seen, flicked my lighter, put the flame to his fag.

'Good boy,' said Dante, 'now take this cigarette out of my mouth and stick it into yours, burning-end first and keep it there until I tell you to take it out.'

'Uh-uh,' I said.

'Either that,' said Fante, 'or we blow a hole in you big enough for the little people at Disneyland to dance through.'

21

'Wait a minute . . .'

'You got 15 seconds,' said Dante, taking out his stopwatch, setting it, then he said, 'Now, you're on. 14, 13, 12, 11 . . .'

'You don't mean it?'

'10, 9, 8, 7, 6, 5, 4, 3 . . .'

I heard the click of a safety catch being taken off.

I snatched the cigarette out of Dante's mouth and stuck it into mine, burning-end first. I tried to engender a mass of saliva and to keep my tongue out of the way, but no luck, I got it, I got it good, it HURT!!!! It was vile and painful! I began to gag and had to spit the thing out.

'Bad boy!' said Dante. 'I told you to keep it in until I told you to take it out! Now we are going to have to start all over again!'

'Fuck you,' I said, 'kill me!'

'OK,' said Dante.

Just then the door opened and Lady Death walked in. She was really dolled up. I almost forgot about my mouth.

'Hey,' said Dante, 'what a babe! You know her, Belane?'

'We've met.'

She walked over to a chair, sat down, crossed her legs, her skirt riding high. None of us could believe those legs. Even I couldn't and I had seen them before.

'Who are these clowns?' she asked me.

'They're emissaries from a guy called Tony.'

'Get 'em out of here, *I'm* your client.'

'All right, fellows,' I said, 'it's time to leave.'

'Oh yeah?' said Dante.

'Oh yeah?' said Fante.

Then they started laughing. Then, all at once, they stopped.

'This guy's real funny,' said Fante.

'Yeah,' said Dante.

'I'll get rid of them,' said Lady Death.

Then she started staring at Dante. At once, he began to lean forward in his chair. He began to look pale.

'Jesus,' he said, 'I don't feel so good . . .'

He turned white, then he turned yellow.

'I feel sick,' he said, 'I feel awful sick . . .'

'Maybe it was those fishsticks you ate,' said Fante.

'Fishsticks, smishsticks, I gotta get out a here! I need a doctor or something . . .'

Then I saw her staring at Fante. Then Fante said, 'I'm getting dizzy . . . What is this? . . . Flashes of light . . . Rocket flares . . . Where am I?'

He moved toward the door, Dante followed him. They opened the door and walked slowly toward the elevator. I walked out and watched them get in. I saw them just before the door closed. They looked horrible. Horrible.

I walked back into the room.

'Thanks,' I said, 'you saved my ass . . .'

I looked around. She was gone. I looked under the desk. Nobody. I looked in the bathroom. Nobody. I opened the window and looked down in the street. Nobody. Well, I mean, there were plenty of people but not her. She could at least have said goodbye. Still, it had been a nice visitation.

I went back and sat behind my desk. Then I picked up the phone and touched in Tony's number.

'Yeah?' he answered, 'this is . . .'

'Tony, this is Mr. Slow Death.'

'What? You still able to talk?'

'I talk real good, Tony. I've never felt better.'

'I don't understand this . . .'

'Your boys were by, Tony . . .'

'Yeah? Yeah?'

'I let them off easy this time. You send them again and I'm going to take them all the way out.'

I heard Tony breathing into the phone. It was a very confused breathing. Then he hung up.

I took a pint of scotch out of the lower left hand drawer, uncapped it and had a good hit.

You messed with Belane, you were in trouble. It was as simple as that.

I capped the bottle, put it back in the drawer and wondered what I was going to do next. A good dick always has things to do. You've seen it in the movies.

9

There was a knock on the door. No, it was 5 rapid knocks, loud, insistent.

I can always take a reading on a knock. Sometimes when I get a bad reading I don't answer.

This knock was only half-bad.

'Come in,' I said.

The door swung open. It was a man, mid-fifties, semiwealthy, semi-nervous, feet too big, wart on upper left forehead, brown eyes, necktie. 2 cars, 2 homes, no children. Pool and spa, he played the stockmarket and was fairly dumb.

He just stood there, sweating just a bit and staring at me.

'Sit down,' I said.

'I'm Jack Bass,' he said, 'and . . .'

'I know.'

'What?'

'You think your wife is copulating with somebody or somebodies.'

'Yes.'

'She's in her twenties.'

'Yes. I want you to prove that she is doing it, then I want a divorce.'

'Why bother, Bass? Just divorce her.'

'I just want to prove that she . . . she . . .'

'Forget it. She'll get just as much money either way. It's the New Age.'

'What do you mean?'

'It's called the no-fault divorce. It doesn't matter what anybody does.'

'How come?'

'It speeds up justice, clears the courts.'

'But that's not justice.'

'They think it is.'

Bass just sat in his chair, breathing, and looking at me.

I had to straighten out the Celine matter and find the Red Sparrow and here was this flabby ball of flesh worried because his wife was screwing somebody.

Then he spoke. 'I just want to find out. I just want to find out for myself.'

'I don't come cheap.'

'How much?'

'6 bucks an hour.'

'That doesn't seem like much money.'

'Does to me. You got a photo of your wife?'

He dug into his wallet, came up with one, handed it to me.

I looked at it.

'Oh my! Does she really look like this?'

'Yes.'

'I'm getting a hard-on just looking at this.'

'Hey, don't be a wise guy!'

'Oh, sorry . . . But I'll have to keep the photo. I'll return it when I'm finished.'

I put it in my wallet.

'Is she still living with you?'

'Yes.'

'And you go to work?'

'Yes.'

'And then, sometimes, she . . .'

'Yes.'

'And what makes you think she . . .'

'Tips, phone calls, voices in my head, her changed behavior, any number of things.'

I pushed a notepad toward him.

'Put down your address, home and business, phone, home and business. I'll take it from there. I'll nail her ass to the wall. I'll uncover the whole thing.'

'What?'

'I am accepting this case, Mr. Bass. Upon its fruition you will be informed.'

' "Fruition"?' he asked. 'Listen, are you all right?'

26

'I'm straight. How about you?'

'Oh yeah, I'm all right.'

'Then don't worry, I'm your man, I'll nail her ass!'

Bass rose slowly from his chair. He moved toward the door, then turned.

'Barton recommended you.'

'There you go then! Good afternoon, Mr. Bass.'

The door closed and he was gone. Good old Barton.

I took her photo out of my wallet and sat there looking at it.

You bitch, I thought, you bitch.

I got up and locked the door, then took the phone off the hook. I sat behind my desk looking at the photo.

You bitch, I thought, I'll nail your ass! Against the wall! No mercy for you! I'll catch you in the act! I'll catch you at it! You whore, you bitch, you whore!

I began breathing heavily. I unzipped. Then the earthquake hit. I dropped the photo and ducked under the desk. It was a good one. Around a 6. Felt like it lasted a couple of minutes. Then it stopped. I crawled out from under the desk, still unzipped. I found the photo again, put it back in my wallet, zipped up. Sex was a trap, a snare. It was for animals. I had too much sense for that kind of crap. I put the phone back on the hook, opened the door, stepped out, locked it and walked down to the elevator. I had work to do. I was the best dick in LA *and* Hollywood. I hit the button and waited for the fucking elevator to come on up.

10

___

Skip the rest of the day and night here, no action, it's not worth talking about.

11

___

The next morning, 8 a.m., I was parked in my VW Bug across from Jack Bass's house. I had a hangover and I was reading the *L.A. Times.* Anyhow, I'd done a bit of research. Bass's wife, her first name was Cindy. Cindy Bass, formerly Cindy Maybell. Her press clippings revealed that she was a small time beauty contest winner, Miss Chili Cook-Off of 1990. Model, bit-part actress, liked to ski, student of the piano, liked baseball and water polo. Favorite color: red. Favorite fruit: banana. Liked to cat nap. Liked children. Liked jazz. Read Kant. Sure. Some day hoped to enter the bar, etc.,

etc. Met Jack Bass over a roulette wheel in Las Vegas. They were married two nights later.

About 8:30 a.m. Jack Bass backed out of his drive in his Mercedes and headed for his executive position at the Aztec Petroleum Corp. Now it was me and Cindy. I was going to bust her wide open. She was at my mercy. I took out the photo for a recheck. I started sweating. I pulled down the sun visor. The whore, she was dumping on Jack Bass.

I slipped the photo back into my wallet. I was beginning to feel eerie. What was wrong with me? Was this dame getting to me? She had intestines like everybody else. She had nostril hairs. She had wax in her ears. What was the big play? Why was the windshield rolling in front of me like a big wave? Must be the hangover. Vodka with beer chaser. You had to pay. Nice thing about being a drunk, though, you were never constipated. Sometimes I thought about my liver but my liver never spoke up, it never said, 'Stop it, you're killing me and I'm going to kill you!' If we had talking livers we wouldn't need A.A.

I sat in the car waiting for Cindy to come out.

It was a sultry summer morning.

I must have fallen asleep, sitting there. I don't know what awakened me. But there was *her* Mercedes backing out of the drive. She swung it around, headed south and I followed her. Red Mercedes. I followed her to the freeway, the San Diego, she took the fast lane and hit it. Well, she was doing 75 anyhow. She must have been hot. She wanted it. I felt something twitch between my legs. A sheath of sweat began to layer my forehead.

She got it up to 80. She was in heat, the bitch was in heat! Cindy, Cindy! I stayed right with her 4 car lengths behind. I'd nail her ass, I'd nail her ass like it had never been nailed before! This was it! Chase and consummation! I was Nick Belane, super dick!

Then I saw the flashing red lights in my rear view mirror.

Shit!

I gradually edged over to the slow lane, saw a shoulder, parked the Bug, got out. The cops stopped 5 car lengths back. One got out on each side. I went toward them, reaching for my wallet. The tall cop flipped his gun out of the holster, pointed it at me.

'Hold it, buddy!'

I stopped. 'What the hell you going to do, drill me? Go ahead, go ahead, *drill me!*'

The shorter one came around behind me, got me in an arm lock, walked me to the hood of the police car and slammed me down over it.

'You shit!' he said. 'You know what we do with pricks like you?'

'Yeah, I got a damned good idea.'

'This prick is a wise guy!' said the short cop.

'Take it easy, Louie,' said the tall cop, 'somebody might have a camcorder. This is not the place.'

'Bill, I hate wise guys!'

'We'll bust him, Louis. We'll bust his ass good later.'

I was still jammed over the hood. Cars were slowing on the freeway. The gawkers were gawking.

'Come on, fellows,' I said, 'we're causing a traffic jam.'

'You think we give a fuck?' asked Bill.

'You threatened us, you ran toward us reaching into your waistband!' screamed Louie.

'I was reaching for my wallet. I wanted to show you my ID. I'm a registered detective, city of Los Angeles. I was tailing a suspect.'

Louie let go the death grip he had on my arm.

'Stand up.'

'OK.'

'Now, slowly reach for your wallet and take out your driver's license.'

'OK.'

I handed him a little slip of paper, folded up.

'What the hell is this?' he asked.

The cop handed it back to me.

'Unfold it, then hand it back.'

I did that, said, 'It's a kind of temporary license. They took my old one when I failed my driver's license test, the written one. This lets me drive until I take my next test in a week.'

'You mean, you flunked your test?'

'Yeah.'

'Hey, Bill, this guy flunked his driver's test!'

'What? Really?'

'I had things on my mind . . .'

'Looks like you had nothing on your mind,' Louie smirked.

'It's for laughs,' said Bill.

'And you mean you're a licensed detective?' asked Louie.

'Yep.'

'Hard to believe.'

'I was hot after a suspect when you flashed your lights. I was just about to nail her ass.'

I handed Louie the photo.

'Holy shit!' he said. He kept staring at the photo. It was a full length shot. She was in a mini-skirt and a low cut blouse, very low cut.

'Hey, Bill, look at this!'

'I was hot on her tail, Bill, I was just about to nail her ass.'

Bill kept staring at the photo.

'Uhhh uhhh uhhh,' he went.

'I need the photo back, officer. Personal evidence.'

'Oh yeah, sure,' he said, reluctantly handing it back.

'Well, we ought to bust you,' said Louie.

'But we won't,' said Bill, 'we'll write you up for doing 75 even though you were doing 80. But we get to keep the photo.'

'What?'

'You heard.'

'But that's extortion!' I said.

Bill moved his hand toward his gun.

'What did you say?'

'I said, it's a deal.'

I handed the photo back to Bill. He began writing out the speeding ticket. I stood there waiting. Then he handed me the ticket.

'Sign it.'

I did.

He ripped it off and handed it to me.

'You've got ten days to pay or if you plead not guilty to appear in court as indicated.'

'Thank you, officer.'

'And drive with care,' said Louie.

'You too, buddy.'

32

'What?'

'I said, sure.'

They strolled back toward their car. I strolled toward mine. I got in, started the engine. They were just sitting back there. I pulled into traffic, then kept it at 60.

Cindy, I thought, you're really going to pay now! I'm going to nail your ass like it has never been nailed!

Then I got to the Harbor Freeway turnoff, took 110 south and just drove along, hardly knowing where I was going.

12

I rode the Harbor Freeway to the end. I was in San Pedro. I drove down Gaffey, took a left on 7th, went a few blocks, took a right on Pacific, just drove along, saw a bar, The Thirst Hog, parked, went on in. It was dark in there. The TV was off. The bartender was an old guy, looked to be 80, all white, white hair, white skin, white lips. Two other old guys sat there, chalk white. Looked like the blood had stopped running in all of them. They reminded me of flies in a spider web, sucked dry. No drinks were showing. Everybody was motionless. A white stillness.

I stood in the doorway looking at them.

Finally the bartender made a sound: 'Etch . . .?'

'Has anybody here seen Cindy, Celine or the Red Sparrow?' I asked.

They just looked at me. One of the patrons' mouths drew together into a little wet hole. He was trying to speak. He couldn't do it. The other patron reached down and scratched his balls. Or where his balls used to be. The bartender remained motionless. He looked like a cardboard cutout. An old one. Suddenly I felt young.

I moved forward and took a bar stool.

'Any chance of getting a drink here?' I asked.

'Etch . . .' said the bartender.

'Vodka 7, forget the lime.'

Now just kick four-and-one-half minutes in the ass and forget it. That's how long it took the bartender to get it to me.

'Thank you,' I said, 'now please make me another while you are in motion.'

I took a hit of the drink. It wasn't bad. He'd had lots of practice.

The two old guys just sat there looking at me.

'Nice day, isn't it fellows?' I asked.

They didn't answer. I got the feeling that they weren't breathing. Weren't you supposed to bury the dead?

'Listen, fellows, when was the last time either one of you pulled down a pair of women's panties?'

One of the old guys started going, 'Heh, heh, heh, heh!'

'Oh, last night, huh?'

'Heh, heh, heh, heh!'

'Was it good?'

'Heh, heh, heh, heh!'

I was getting depressed. My life wasn't going anywhere. I needed something, the flashing of lights,
glamour, some damn thing. And here I was, talking to
the dead.

I finished my first drink. The second was ready.

Two guys walked through the doorway wearing
stocking masks.

I downed my second drink.

'ALL RIGHT! NO SHIT FROM ANYBODY! WALLETS, RINGS
AND WATCHES ON THE BAR! NOW!' screamed one guy.

The other guy leaped over the bar and ran to the cash
register. He pounded at it.

'HEY! HOW DO YOU OPEN THIS FUCKING THING?'

He looked around, saw the bartender. 'HEY, GRAMPS!
COME HERE AND OPEN THIS THING!' He pointed his gun at
him. All of a sudden the bartender knew how to move.
He was at the register in a wink and had it open.

The other guy was putting the stuff we had laid on
the bar into a sack.

'GET THE CIGAR BOX! UNDER THE BAR!' he yelled at his
buddy.

The guy behind the bar was stuffing the cash from the
register into a sack. He found the cigar box. It was
loaded. He stuffed it in the sack and leaped over the
bar.

Then they both stood there for a moment.

'I *feel kind of crazy*!' said the guy who had leaped
over the bar.

'Forget it, we're leaving!' said the other guy.

'I FEEL CRAZY!' yelled the first guy. He pointed his gun
at the bartender. He fired three shots. All into the gut.
The old man jerked three times, then fell.

'YOU FUCKING FOOL! WHAT DID YOU DO THAT FOR?' his cohort yelled.

'DON'T CALL ME A FOOL! I'LL KILL YOU TOO!' he screamed, then turned and pointed his gun at his partner. He was too late. The shot went through his nose and came out the back of his head. He fell over taking a bar stool down with him. The other guy ran out the door. I counted to five, then ran out after him. The two old guys were still alive when I left. I think.

I was in my car fast. I dug out from the curb, went a block, took a right and went down a back street. Then I slowed down and drove along. I heard a siren then. I lit a cigarette from the dash, turned the radio on. I got some rap music. I couldn't understand what the guy was rapping about.

I didn't know whether to go back to my place or the office.

I ended up in a supermarket pushing along a cart. I got 5 grapefruit, a roasted chicken and some potato salad. A fifth of vodka and some toilet paper.

13

I found myself back at my apartment. I dove into the chicken and the potato salad. I rolled a grapefruit across the rug. I felt frustrated. Everything was defeating me.

Then the phone rang. I spit out a half-cooked chicken wing and answered.

'Yeah?'

'Mr. Belane?'

'Yeah?'

'You've won a free trip to Hawaii,' somebody said.

I hung up. I walked into the kitchen and poured a vodka with mineral water plus a touch of tabasco sauce. I sat down with it, had half a hit, then there was a knock on the door. I got a bad read on the knock, but I went ahead anyhow and said, 'Come on in.'

Much to my regret. It was my neighbor from 302, the mailman. His arms always hung kind of funny. His mind too. His eyes never quite looked at you but somewhere over your head. Like you were back there instead of where you were. There were a few other things wrong with him too.

'Hey, Belane, got a drink for me?'

'In the kitchen, mix your own.'

'Sure.'

He walked into the kitchen, whistling Dixie.

Then he came sauntering out, a drink in each hand. He sat down across from me.

'Didn't want to run short,' he said, nodding at his drinks.

'You know,' I informed him, 'they sell that stuff in a lot of places. You ought to stock up.'

'Forget that . . . look, Belane, I'm here to talk turkey.'

He drained the drink in his right hand, smashed the glass against the wall. He'd learned that from me.

'Look, Belane, I'm here to start us both on the road to easy glory.'

'Sure,' I said, 'let's hear it.'

'Loco Mike. Ran the other day. Speed like a leper's tongue on a virgin tit – ran the first quarter in 21.0. Came blazing into the stretch with a 5 length lead, 20 thousand dollar claimers, only got beat by a length and a half. Now he's dropping down against 15 thousand claimers. Rabbit like that, at 6 furlongs. All they'll see is his asshole. The *Racing Form* has him listed at 15 to 1! A steal! I'm cutting you in on the action, good buddy!'

'Why cut me in? Why don't you take *all* the action?'

He drained his other drink. Then looked around. Raised his glass.

'Hold it!' I said. 'You smash that glass and you're going to have two assholes.'

'Huh?'

'Think about it.'

The mailman quietly set his glass down.

'Got any more to drink?'

'You know it. Pour me one too.'

He walked into the kitchen. I felt myself gradually losing my patience.

Then he came out, handed a drink to me.

'Hold it,' I said, 'I'll take your drink.'

'How come?'

'It's stronger.'

He handed me the other drink, then sat down.

'Now like I said, mailbag, why cut me in?'

'Well, ha,' he said.

'Yes, go on . . .'

'I'm a little short of green. Got nothing to put down. But after we score I can pay you from the profits.'

'I don't like the sound of that.'

'Look, Belane, I just need a little scratch.'

'How much?'

'20 bucks.'

'That's a hell of a lot of money.'

'10 bucks.'

'10 fucking bucks?'

'OK, 5 bucks.'

'What?'

'2 bucks.'

'Drag your sack out of here!'

He drained his drink and stood up. I finished mine. He just stood there.

He said, 'How come all these grapefruits are on the floor?'

'Because I like them like that.'

I got up and moved toward him.

'Time to go, fellow.'

'Time to go, huh? I'll go when I'm damn good and ready!'

The drinks had made him bold. That happens.

I slammed my fist into his gut. I had on my brass knuckles. Damn near went right through him.

He dropped.

I walked over and scooped up some broken glass from the floor. Then I came back, opened his mouth and dropped the glass in there. Then I rubbed his cheeks around and slapped him up a bit. His lips turned redder.

Then I went about my business of drinking. I suppose about 45 minutes passed and the mailman began to move. He rolled over, spit out a shard of glass and began crawling toward the door. He looked pitiful. He crawled right up to the door. I opened it and he crawled out and down toward his apartment. I'd have to watch him in the future.

I closed the door.

I sat down and found half a dead cigar in the ashtray. I lit it up, took a drag, gagged. Tried it again. Not too bad.

I felt introspective.

I decided not to do any more that day.

Life wore a man out, wore a man thin.

Tomorrow would be a better day.

14

The next day I was back at Red's bookstore. I was on the Celine case again. The racetrack was closed and it was a cloudy day. Red was marking up the prices on some rare items.

'How about Musso's?' he asked.

'I can't, Red. I seem to be eating all the time. Look at me.'

I pulled back my coat. My gut was pushing out through my shirt. A button had popped off.

'You better get that fat sucked out. You'll have a heart attack. They suck the fat out through a tube. You can put it in a jar and look at it, it'll remind you to lay off the jelly donuts.'

'I'll think about it. You want some grapefruit?'

'Grapefruit? That's not fattening.'

'I know but I fell over one when I got up this morning, they're dangerous.'

'Where'd you sleep, in the refrigerator?'

I sighed.

'Look, let's change the subject. You know this guy who looks like Celine?'

'Oh, him . . .'

'Him. He been in lately?'

'Not since you were here. You trailing this bird?'

'You might say so.'

Then, just like that, he walked in. Celine.

He slid past us and went down the aisle and plucked up a book.

I walked over close to him. Real close. He had the signed copy of *As I Lay Dying*. Then he noticed me.

'In the old days,' he said, 'writers' lives were more interesting than their writing. Now-a-days neither the lives nor the writing is interesting.'

He slid Faulkner back into place.

'You live around here?' I asked.

'Maybe. How about you?'

'You once had a French accent, didn't you?' I asked.

'Maybe. How about you?'

'Oh, nothing like that. Listen, did anybody ever tell you that you resembled somebody else?'

'We all, more or less, resemble somebody else. Look, do you have a cigarette?'

'Of course.'

I dug for my pack.

'Please,' he said, 'take one and light it, smoke it. It will keep you busy.'

He began to walk away.

I lit my cigarette, took a drag. Then I followed him. I gave Red a goodbye nod, then stepped into the street. Just in time to see him get into an '89 Fiat at the curb. And who was parked right behind him? My Bug was parked right behind him. What luck! Talk about fornicating the odds! First time I had found curb parking in months! I leaped in, gunned out and followed him.

He went east down Hollywood Boulevard.

Lady Death, I thought, watch me, at your service.

Then I almost lost him at the next signal, but I sliced through the beginning of a red light. No problem except for a little old lady in a Caddy who called me a dirty name. I smiled.

Soon Celine and I were on the Hollywood Freeway as the sun burned through the clouds. I kept Celine in my sights. I felt good. Maybe I'd get the fat sucked out through a tube. I was still a young man. My life was before me.

Then Celine was on the Harbor Freeway.

Then he was on the Santa Monica.

Then he was on the San Diego. South.

Then Celine took a turnoff and I followed him along. The territory seemed to look familiar. I followed along about half a block back. I hoped he wasn't checking his rear view too much.

Then I saw him slow, pull over and stop. I slid over to the curb, parked and watched.

He got out of his car and walked down a few houses, then he crossed the street while looking over his shoulder. He stopped, looked around again, then went up a walkway to this house. He stepped onto the porch, looked around and knocked. It was a large house and had a familiar look.

The door opened and Celine went inside.

I pulled away from the curb and slowly drove by. It was Jack Bass's place. Say that real fast. It was only 2:30 p.m. Cindy's red Mercedes was parked in the drive.

I circled the block and parked at my old spot.

I was going to kill two birds with one stone. I was going to uncover Celine and I was going to nail Cindy's ass.

I'd give them some time. Ten minutes.

When I was in grammar school we had a lady teacher who asked us, 'What do you want to be when you grow up?' And almost all the boys said they wanted to be firemen. That was dumb, you could get burned. A few guys said they wanted to be doctors or lawyers but nobody said, 'I want to be a detective.' And now, here I was one. Oh, when she came to me I said, 'I dunno . . .'

The ten minutes were up. I grabbed my mini-camcorder, kicked the car door open and moved toward the house. I felt myself trembling a bit, inhaled deeply and stepped up to the door. The door lock was no problem. Within 45 seconds I was inside.

I walked down the hall, then I heard voices. I walked up to a door. They were in there. I heard their voices. Their tones were low. I pressed forward and listened.

I heard Celine.

'You need this . . . you know it . . .'

'I. . .' I heard Cindy, 'I'm not sure . . . Suppose Jack finds out?'

'He'll never know . . .'

'Jack is a violent man . . .'

'He'll never know. This is for your own good . . .'

Cindy laughed.

'My good . . .? Won't you get anything out of it?'

'Of course . . . Here, here, look, take this in your hand . . . It's a beginning . . .'

I waited a few seconds, then I kicked the door open and swung in there with my camcorder. I had it on and focused.

They were sitting over a coffee table and Cindy appeared to be signing some papers. She looked up and screamed.

'Oh shit,' I said.

I lowered the camcorder.

'What the hell is this?' Celine asked. 'You know this guy?'

'I never saw him before!'

'I have,' said Celine. 'He hangs around this bookstore asking me stupid questions.'

'I'm going to call the police!' Cindy said.

'Hold it,' I said, 'I can explain everything!'

'It better be good,' said Cindy.

'It better,' said Celine.

I couldn't think of anything. I just stood there.

'I'm going to call the police,' said Cindy, 'now!'

'Hold it,' I said. 'Your husband, Jack Bass, he hired me. I'm a dick.'

'Hired you? For what?'

'To nail your ass.'

'To nail my ass?'

'Yes.'

'I was just trying to sell this lady some insurance,' said Celine, 'and you come busting in here with your camera.'

'I'm sorry, it was an error. Please allow me to rectify it.'

'How the hell are you going to rectify this?' asked Celine.

'I don't know right now. I'm terribly sorry. I'll find something to make all this better. Really.'

'This guy is some kind of jerk,' said Cindy, 'a mental case!'

'I'm sorry. But I'm going to leave now. I'll contact you about everything.'

'We're going to turn you over to the police!' stated Cindy.

'I must be leaving,' I said.

'Oh, no!' said Cindy, 'you're not going anywhere!'

She hit a buzzer as I turned to move out through the door. But there stood a reasonable facsimile of King Kong. He was monstrous. He moved slowly toward me.

'Hey, boy,' I asked him, 'do you like candy?'

'Punk,' he said, 'you're my candy!'

'How about some toys? What kinda toys you like?'

King Kong ignored that. He turned to Cindy.

'You want me to kill him?'

'No, Brewster, just fix him so he can't move around so well for a while.'

'OK.'

He moved toward me.

'Brewster,' I said, 'who did you vote for President?'

'Huh?'

He stopped to think.

I took the mini-camcorder and hurled it straight at his playground. It slammed in on target. He bent over, grabbed his privates.

I ran forward, picked up the camcorder and brought it down on the back of his neck. I heard glass breaking.

King Kong toppled over. He fell face forward on the couch, out cold. Half his body was on the couch, the other part somewhere else.

I stepped forward and picked up what was left of the camcorder.

I looked at Cindy.

'I'm still going to nail your ass.'

'This man is crazy!' she yelled.

'I believe that you are right,' said Celine.

I spun on my heel and got the hell out of there.

Another wasted day.

15

The next day I was in my office. Everything seemed to be at a dead end. It had been a terrible night, I had tried to drink myself to sleep. But the walls to my apartment were thin. I had heard everything next door . . .

'Hey, baby, this turkeyneck is loaded with sticky white paste and it's got to get out or I'm gonna have a stroke or something!'

'That's your problem, buster.'

'But we're married!'

'You're too ugly.'

'What? Huh? You never told me.'

'I just decided.'

'Well, the cream's rising to my ears, baby! I gotta do something!'

'You'll do it without me, Jackhammer!'

'OK. OK. Where's the cat?'

'The cat? Oh no, you bastard, *not Tinker Bell*!'

'Where's that god damned cat? I just saw it a minute ago!'

'Don't you dare! Don't you dare! *Not Tinker Bell*!'

I hadn't been able to drink myself to sleep. I had just sat there, pouring them down. No luck.

And now, like I said, it was the next morning, back at the office. I felt totally useless. I was useless. There were billions of women out there and not one of them was making her way toward my door. Why? I was a loser. I was a dick who couldn't solve anything.

I watched the fly crawling across my desk and I got ready to take it into the darkness.

Then there was a flash of light!

I leaped up.

Celine was selling Cindy *insurance*! *Life insurance* on Jack Bass! Now they were going to take him out, make it look natural! They were in it together! I had them by the balls. Well, I had Celine by the balls and Cindy –

well, I'd nail her ass. Jack Bass was in trouble. And Lady Death wanted Celine. And the Red Sparrow still had not been found. But I felt myself moving toward something. Something big. I took my hand out of my pocket and picked up the telephone. Then I put it down. Who the hell did I think I was going to call? I knew what time it was. And Jack Bass was in deep. I had to think. I tried to think. The fly was still crawling along the desk. I rolled up the *Racing Form*, took a swat at it and missed. It wasn't my day. My week. My month. My year. My life. God damn it.

I sat back in my chair. Born to die. Born to live like a harried chipmunk. Where were the chorus girls? Why did I feel like I was attending my own funeral?

The door swung open. And there stood Celine.

'You,' I said, 'it had to be you.'

'I know the song,' he said.

'Don't you ever knock?'

'Depends,' said Celine. 'Mind if I sit down?'

'Yes, but go ahead.'

He reached into my cigar box, took one out, unpeeled it, bit off the end, took out a lighter, lit up, inhaled, then exhaled a gorgeous plume of smoke.

'They sell those things, you know,' I told him.

'What don't they sell?'

'Air. But they will. Now, what do you want?'

'Well, good buddy . . .'

'Cut the crap.'

'All right, all right . . . Well, let's see . . .'

Celine placed his feet up on my desk.

'Nice shoes you got there,' I told him. 'You buy them in France?'

'France, Schmantz, who cares?'

He exhaled another plume of smoke.

'Why are you here?' I asked.

'Good question,' he said. 'It has thundered down through the centuries.'

' "Thundered"?'

'Don't be so picky for Christ's sake. You act like a guy who had an unhappy childhood.'

I yawned.

'So,' he said, 'it's like this. You're in deep shit on at least two counts. Breaking and entering. Assault and battery . . .'

'What?'

'Brewster is now a eunuch. You crushed his balls with that camcorder, they look like a couple of dried figs. Now he can sing ultra-soprano.'

'And?'

'We know the whereabouts of the culprit who broke and entered, who eliminated the manhood of another.'

'And?'

'And it is possible that the police might be informed.'

'You got any real evidence?'

'Three witnesses.'

'That's a bunch.'

Celine took his feet down, leaned over the desk close to me, staring directly into my eyes.

'Belane, I need a loan of ten grand.'

'I got it. *I got it! Blackmail! You swine! Blackmail!*'

I felt myself getting excited. It felt pretty good.

'It's not blackmail, sucker. I am only asking you for a loan of ten grand. A loan, got it?'

'A loan? You got any collateral?'

'Hell no.'

I stood up behind my desk.

'You god-damned snail! You think I am going to hold still for this?'

I moved around the desk toward him.

'BREWSTER!' he yelled, 'NOW!'

The door opened and in strolled my old friend, Brewster.

'Hi, Mr. Belane!' he said in a high pitched voice. But it didn't make him any smaller. He was the biggest son of a bitch I had ever seen. I walked around behind my desk, slid open the drawer and pulled out the .45. I leveled it at him.

'Sonny boy,' I said, 'this thing can stop a train! You wanna pretend you're a choo-choo? Come on, come on, choo-choo! You come along the tracks toward me! I'm gonna derail you! Come on, choo-choo! Come on!'

I flipped the safety catch off and aimed for his massive gut.

Brewster stopped.

'I don't like this game . . .'

'OK,' I said, 'now see that door over there?'

'Uh huh . . .'

'That's the bathroom door. Now I want you to go in there and sit on the potty. I don't give a damn if you pull your pants down or not. But I want you to go in there and sit on the potty until I tell you to come out!'

'OK.'

He walked over to the door, opened it, closed it and then he was in there. What a pitiful mass of dangerous nothing.

Then I pointed the .45 at Celine.

'You,' I said.

'You're fucking up, Belane . . .'

'I always fuck up. Now, you . . . get in there with your boy. Go on, now . . . move!'

Celine put out his cigar, then slowly moved toward the crapper door. I followed along behind him. I goosed him with the .45.

'Get on in there!'

He walked in and closed the door. I took out my key and locked it. Then I went to my desk and slowly began pushing it toward the crapper door. It was a very heavy desk. I had to go inch by inch. It was hell. It took me ten minutes to move it 15 feet. Then it was shoved directly against the door.

'Belane,' I heard Celine say through the door, 'you let us out now and we'll call it even. I won't need the loan. I won't go to the heat. Brewster won't hurt you. And I'll take care of Cindy.'

'Hey, baby,' I said, '*I'll* take care of Cindy! I'm going to nail her ass!'

I left them there. I locked the office door, walked down the hall and took the elevator down. Suddenly I felt better about everything. The elevator hit the first floor and I walked out into the street. First bum who hit on me, I gave him a dollar. I told the second bum I had just given another bum a dollar. Third bum, same thing, etc. There wasn't even any smog that day. I moved forward with a purpose. I had decided on lunch: shrimp and fries. My feet looked good moving along the pavement.

16

After I ate I parked a quarter of a block from Cindy's. There was her red Mercedes parked in the drive. She was probably waiting for Celine and Brewster to return. Too bad. I turned on the radio for some news.

'You fool,' a voice came from the radio, 'you aren't making any progress!'

'Who, me?' I asked.

'You're the only one sitting here, aren't you?'

I looked around. 'Yes,' I said, 'I'm the only one.'

'Then get your ass hopping!'

It was the voice of Lady Death coming through the radio.

'Listen, baby, I'm working on the case now. I'm on a stake-out.'

'Who are you staking out?'

'A connection of Celine's. It all ties together.'

'So do your shoes. Where's Celine?'

'In a crapper with a 400 pound eunuch.'

'What's he doing there?'

'I'm letting him cool off.'

'I don't want him hurt. He's mine.'

'I won't hurt him, baby, honest injun!'

'Sometimes, Belane, I think you're some kind of subnormal.'

'OVER AND OUT!' I screamed and snapped the radio off.

Then I just sat there looking at the red Mercedes and thinking of Cindy. I had my backup mini-camcorder with me. I began to feel hot for the action. The thought occurred to me that I might slip into the premises and pick up on something. Maybe I could catch one of her conversations on the telephone. Maybe I would stumble onto some clue. Sure, it was dangerous. Broad daylight. But I thrived on danger. It made my ears tingle and my butthole pucker. You only live once, right? Well, except for Lazarus. Poor sucker, he had to die twice. But I was Nick Belane. You only rode the merry-go-round once. Life was for the daring.

I slipped out of my car with my mini-camcorder. And I also carried my briefcase as a ploy. I tipped my derby low over my left eye and moved toward the house. My inner sensor was on fully. Something was going on in that house. I felt it strongly. I even bit my tongue in the excitement. I spit out some blood and moved toward the door. Again, it was no problem. 47 seconds and I was inside.

I moved down the hall with my ears pricked. I began to think I was hearing voices. I was. A man's and a woman's. I paused at the bottom of the stairway. Yes, the voices came from upstairs. I moved slowly up the stairway. I heard the voices much better. One I recognized as Cindy's. I kept moving forward, then stopped outside the door. It was evidently a bedroom door. I pressed closer.

I heard Cindy laughing. 'What do you think you're going to do with that thing?'

'One guess, baby! I've been waiting a long time!'

'Well, you came to the right place, big boy!'

'I'm going to ride you all the way to hell and back, baby!'

'Oh yeah?'

'You bitch!'

I heard Cindy laughing again. Then it got quiet. It stayed quiet for a little while. Then it began to get noisy. I heard hard breathing and a slight thumping sound, plus the working of bed springs.

'Oh!' I heard Cindy. 'Oh, my god!'

I put the briefcase down, turned on the camcorder, kicked the door open.

'I'VE NAILED YOUR ASS!'

'WHAT?' the guy looked around from his position. Cindy's legs came down and she SCREAMED.

The guy leaped to the floor and faced me. Horrible looking fat son-of-a-bitch.

'WHAT THE FUCK IS THIS?' he yelled.

It was Jack Bass. For Christ's sake, it was Jack Bass! I spun around and ran down the stairway.

'HOLY SHIT!' I yelled.

I was moving toward the door. As I yanked it open, out of the side of my eye, I saw Jack Bass standing there, balls naked. He had an object in his hand. A gun. He fired. The bullet spun the derby around on my head. He fired again. I felt death rush by my right ear. Then I was sprinting down the sidewalk. I dashed into the street toward my car. Too late, I saw something in the way: an old man on a bicycle pedalling along and eating an apple. I smashed right through him leaving him twisted within the spinning wheels of his bike, upon the asphalt.

I was into the Bug in a flash. I went screeching from the curb. The old man was slowly getting up. I swerved to miss him, jumped the curbing and was onto the sidewalk. Then I was blazing past Jack Bass's place. He was standing in the doorway, still balls naked and he got off 3 more shots. One went right through the monkey hanging from my rear view mirror. The second passed between me and nowhere. The third came through the back of the front seat, passenger's side, hit the glove compartment, and made a hole.

Then I was out of there. I zigzagged up and down a half a dozen side streets. Then I found a boulevard and drove along with the traffic. It was a typical Los Angeles day: smog, a half-sun and no rain for months.

I pulled into a McDonald's, ordered a large fries, coffee and an order of chicken-on-a-bun.

17

I went back to the office. Brewster and Celine had broken out of the crapper. The crapper door was smashed open. I pushed my desk back. It took me 15 minutes.

I sat down and tried to piece everything together.

Now everybody was after my ass: Celine, Brewster, Cindy, Jack Bass and Lady Death. Maybe even Barton. I was no longer sure who my clients were or if I even had any.

I could be arrested for any number of recent offenses. Or somebody could come to get me. The office was a dangerous place to be. I checked my holster for the .45. Still there. Nice baby. Well, they weren't going to run me out of my office. A dick without an office wasn't a dick.

And I didn't know if Celine *was* Celine and I hadn't found the Red Sparrow. Nothing was moving.

It had been a long day. I put my feet up on the desk and leaned back in the chair and closed my eyes. Soon I was asleep.

In my dream I was sitting in this cheap bar. I was having a double whiskey and soda. I was the only one in the bar except the barkeep who seemed rather indistinct. He just stood at the other end of the bar reading *The National Enquirer*. Then a really crappy and dissolute sort walked in. He needed a shave, he needed a haircut, he needed a bath. He was dressed in a dirty yellow raincoat which came down to his shoetops. Under the raincoat you could see a white T-shirt and a faded orange tie. He moved toward me like a stinking wind. He took the stool next to mine. I had a hit of my drink. The bartender looked over. He caught my eye.

'I'm hungry,' the barkeep said. 'I'm so hungry I could eat a horse.'

'I wish you'd eat some of those I've bet on,' I told him.

No wonder he looked indistinct. There wasn't much to him. He was as thin as a rail. His cheeks sagged, paper thin. I looked away.

The other guy was still on the stool next to me.

'Psst . . .' he went.

I ignored him. I looked back at the bartender.

'Listen,' I said to him, 'I'll finish my drink and you can lock up, go some place and get something to eat.'

'Thanks,' he said, 'I got to keep this place open. I'll be all right. I'll think of something.'

'Psst . . .' the guy next to me went again.

'Get off my ear, buddy,' I told him.

'I got some info . . .'

'Don't need it. I read the papers.'

'It's info that ain't in the papers.'

'Like what?'

'The Red Sparrow.'

'Hey, barkeep!' I yelled, 'a drink for this gentleman! Give him a rum and coke!'

The barkeep worked at it.

'You live in Redondo Beach?' the guy asked me.

'East Hollywood.'

'Know a guy, looks just like you, he lives in Redondo Beach.'

'That so?'

'Yep.'

The guy's drink arrived. He drained it right off.

'I had a brother,' he said, 'lived in Glendale. Killed himself.'

'He look like you?' I asked.

'Uh huh.'

'Then it figures.'

'I got a sister, lives in Burbank.'

'Cut the crap.'

'It ain't crap.'

'I want to hear about the Red Sparrow.'

'Sure. I'll put you right on it.'

'Well?'

'I'm thirsty . . .'

'Barkeep!' I yelled. 'Another rum and coke for this gentleman!'

The guy waited for his drink. It arrived. He slammed it down. Then he turned and looked at me with his beady, bleary, vacant eyes.

'I got the Sparrow right on me,' he said.

'What?'

'I mean, I got it in my pocket.'

'Great! Let's see it!'

He fumbled around in a pocket. He kept fumbling.

'Hmmm . . . can't seem to find it . . .'

'You prick! You took me! I'm going to bust your sack!'

'I know I had it somewhere . . .'

'I'm going to uncoil your springs, jerko!'

'Wait . . . wait . . . something here . . . yes. In my other pocket . . . I was looking in the wrong pocket . . .'

'Yeah?'

'Yeah, look . . . here . . . here it is . . . the Red Sparrow!'

He pulled it out of his pocket and placed it on the bar. I looked. It was a dead pigeon.

'That's a dead pigeon!' I said.

'No,' he said, 'that's the Red Sparrow.'

I put some bills on the bar for the drinks, then I stood up and gathered the guy up by the collar of his filthy raincoat. I hustled him toward the door, opened it and threw him out into the street. Then I turned back to close the door. And I saw the bartender. He had the pigeon in his hands and was eating it, gnawing at it. His mouth was full of feathers and blood. He winked at me.

Then my desk phone rang and I awakened.

18

I picked up the phone.

'Belane Detective Agency. . . .'

'My name is Grovers, Hal Grovers, I need your help. The police laugh at me.'

'What is it, Mr. Grovers?'

'A space alien is after me.'

'Ha, ha, ha, Mr. Grovers, come on now . . .'

'You see, everybody laughs at me!'

'Sorry Grovers. But before you talk to me any more I gotta tell you my fee.'

'What is it?'

'6 dollars an hour.'

'That doesn't seem to be a problem.'

'No rubber checks or you'll be carrying your walnuts in a sack, got it?'

'Money is not my problem,' he said, 'it's this woman.'

'What woman, Grovers?'

'Hell, the one we're talking about, this space alien.'

'The space alien is a woman?'

'Yeah, yeah . . .'

'How do you know this?'

'She told me.'

'You believe her?'

'Sure, I've seen her do things.'

'Like what?'

'Well, float up through the ceiling, things like that . . .'

'You a drinking man, Grovers?'

'Sure. How about you?'

'Wouldn't do without it . . . Now, listen, Grovers, before we go any further you'll have to get down here in person. It's the third floor of the Ajax Building. Knock before you enter.'

'Any special knock?'

'Yeah, Shave-and-a-Haircut, Six-Bits, then I'll know it's you . . .'

'All right, Mr. Belane . . .'

I killed four flies while waiting. Damn, death was everywhere. Man, bird, beast, reptile, rodent, insect, fish didn't have a chance. The fix was in. I didn't know what to do about it. I got depressed. You know, I see a box boy at the supermarket, he's packing my groceries, then I see him sticking himself into his own grave along with the toilet paper, the beer and the chicken breasts.

Then the secret knock came at the door and I said, 'Please enter, Mr. Grovers.'

He walked in. Not much to him. Four feet eight, 158 pounds, 38 years old, greengray eyes with a tic in the left eye, small ugly yellow mustache, same color as hair which was thinning on top of his too round head. He walked with his toes out, sat down.

We sat looking at each other. That's all we did. Five minutes went by. Finally I got pissed.

'Grovers, why don't you say something?'

'I was waiting for you to speak first.'

'Why?'

'I don't know.'

I leaned back in my chair, lit a cigar, put my feet on the table, inhaled, exhaled, and blew out a perfect smoke ring.

'Grovers, this woman, this . . . space alien . . . tell me a bit about her . . .'

'She calls herself Jeannie Nitro . . .'

'Tell me more, Mr. Grovers.'

'You won't laugh at me like the police did?'

'Nobody laughs like the police, Mr. Grovers.'

'Well . . . she's a hot number from outer space.'

'Why do you want to get rid of a hot number?'

'I'm afraid of her, she controls my mind.'

'Like how?'

'Like anything she says, I have to do.'

'Suppose she told you to eat your poo-poo, would you do that?'

'I think I would . . .'

'Grovers, you're just pussy-whipped. Lot of men like that.'

'No, it's the tricks she does, they're frightening.'

'I've seen all the tricks, Grovers, and then some . . .'

'You haven't seen her appear out of nowhere, you haven't seen her vanish through the ceiling.'

'You're boring me, Grovers, this is a bunch of crap.'

'No, it ain't, Mr. Belane.'

' "Ain't"? Where the hell you come from Grovers? You talk like a backwoodsman.'

'And you don't look like a detective, Mr. Belane.'

'Huh? What? Then what do I look like?'

'Well, let's see, let me think . . .'

'Don't take too fucking long. This is costing you 6 dollars an hour.'

'Well, you look like . . . a plumber.'

'A plumber? A plumber. OK. What would you do without a plumber? Can you think of anybody more important than a plumber?'

'The president.'

'The president? There you go, wrong! Wrong again! Everytime you open your mouth you say something wrong!'

'I'm not wrong.'

'There you see! You did it again!'

I put out my cigar and lit a cigarette. This guy was a pure piece of crap. But he was a client. I looked at him a long time. It was hard work looking at him. I stopped looking. I looked over his left ear.

'OK what do you want me to do? With this space alien? This Jeannie Nitro?'

'Get rid of her.'

'I'm no hit man, Grovers.'

'Just get her out of my life one way or the other.'

'You had sex yet?'

'You mean today?'

'I mean, with *her*.'

'No.'

'You got a place of residence on this bimbo?

Phone number? Occupation? Tattoo? Hobby? Peculiar habits?'

'Only the last . . .'

'Like what?'

'Like she floats through the ceiling and all that.'

'Grovers, you're crazy. You don't need me, you need a shrink.'

'I've been to the shrinks.'

'And what do they say?'

'Nothing. Only they charge more than 6 dollars an hour.'

'What do they charge?'

'One-hundred-seventy-five dollars an hour.'

'That proves you're crazy.'

'Why?'

'Anybody pays that has got to be crazy.'

Then we just sat there looking at each other. It seemed pretty dumb. I was trying to think. My temples hurt.

Then the door swung open. And in walked this woman. Now all that I can tell you is that there are billions of women on earth, right? Some look all right. Most look pretty good. But every now and then nature pulls a wild trick, she puts together a special woman, an unbelievable woman. I mean, you look and you can't believe. Everything is perfect undulating motion, quick-silver, snake like, you see an ankle, you see an elbow, you see a breast, you see a knee, it all melds into a giant, taunting totality, with such beautiful eyes smiling, the mouth turned down a bit, the lips held there as if they were about to burst into laughter over your helpless-ness. And they know how to dress and their long hair burns the air. Too god-damned much.

Grovers stood up.

'Jeannie!'

She glided into the room like a strip teaser on roller skates. She paused before us as the walls trembled. She looked at Grovers.

'Hal, what are you doing with this 2nd rate dick?'

'Hey, hold it, bitch!' I said.

'Well, Jeannie, I got a little problem and I thought I might seek some help.'

'Help? From who?'

'Can't say. Cat's got my tongue.'

'Hal, you've got no problem as long as you have me. I can do anything better than this 2nd rate dick.'

I stood up. I was standing up anyhow.

'Yeah, wench? Let's see you get a 7 inch hard-on.'

'Sexist pig!'

'See, I gotcha, *gotcha*!'

Jeannie wallowed about the room a bit, driving us all mad. Then she swung around. Looked at Grovers.

'Come here, dog! Crawl across the floor toward me! Now!'

'*Don't do it, Hal*!' I screamed.

'Huh?'

He was crawling across the floor toward Jeannie. He got closer and closer. He crawled up to her feet, then stopped.

'Now,' she said, 'lick the toes of my shoes with your tongue!'

Grovers did it. He licked away. He kept going. Jeannie looked at me and smirked. A real smirking smirk. I couldn't handle it.

I leaped up.

'YOU FUCKING WHORE!' I screamed.

I unbuckled my belt, slipped it from my pants, walked around the desk with the belt doubled up.

'You fucking whore,' I said, 'I AM GOING TO NAIL YOUR ASS!'

I rushed toward her. What was left of my soul quivered in a joyous excitement. Her miraculous buns blazed in my mind. Heaven turned upside-down and quivered.

'Drop that belt, jerkoff,' she said, snapping her fingers.

The belt dropped out of my hand. I stood frozen.

She turned to Grovers.

'Come on, silly boy, get up off your knees. We are leaving this stupid place.'

'Yes, darling.'

Grovers got up and followed her to the door, it opened, closed and they were gone. I still couldn't move. The bitch must have used a ray gun on me. And I was still frozen. Maybe I had chosen the wrong profession? After about twenty minutes I began to feel a tingling all through my body. Then I found that I could move my eyebrows. Next my mouth.

'God damn it,' I said.

Then the other parts began to gradually loosen up. Finally I took one step. Two steps. Then more steps, toward my desk. I got around behind it. Opened a drawer. Found the pint of vodka. Unscrewed it. Had a good straight hit. Decided to call it a day and begin all over again tomorrow.

19

Back at the office, the next day, I was confused. I didn't know who my clients were or what the hell. I decided to do something about it. I had the business number of Jack Bass. I rang him.

'Hello,' he said.

'Bass, this is Belane.'

'You son-of-a-bitch.'

'Take it easy, Bass, I got a black belt.'

'You'll need it next time you bust in on one of my love sessions.'

'Jack, all I saw was a bobbing ass. I didn't know it was you until you turned your head.'

'Who else do you think it was? You think some guy is going to slam her in my own home?'

'It's been done plenty of times.'

'What?'

'I don't mean your place, Jack.'

'Where then?'

'It doesn't matter.'

'What doesn't matter?'

'I mean, it doesn't relate to your case. Let's talk turkey.'

'What?'

'You want me on this case or not?'

'You're not getting anywhere, just videoing my butt.'

'I'm right on your case, Jack.'

'Like what?'

'I got a tie-in.'

'What?'

'I got a link.'

' "Tie-in?" "Link?" What are you talking about?'

'I can tie her in with this guy. I know him. A shady sort. They are up to no good.'

'You caught them together?'

'Not yet.'

'Why not?'

'I'm moving slow. I'm going to let them trap themselves.'

'Can't you nail them now?'

'I got to wait until he rings the gong.'

'What?'

'Got to catch them in the act.'

'I don't know if you know what you're doing, Belane.'

'I know exactly what I'm doing. I'll nail him as soon as he rings the gong.'

'I wish you wouldn't talk that way.'

'The world is no kindergarten, Jack. I'm trying to get down on this case.'

'Get down?'

'I want to nail her ass. You want me to nail her ass, don't you?'

'Just get me some proof.'

'The proof is in the pudding, Bass.'

'You getting close to something, Belane?'

'I can smell it, I can sniff it, I'm hot on the trail. I know this guy. He's a Frenchman. And you know about Frenchmen, don't you?'

'No, what about Frenchmen?'

'If you don't know, Bass, I can't tell you. I don't have all day. Now, do you want me to follow up on this god-damned case or not?'

'You say you're closing in?'

'I'm right on top of both of them.'

'What?'

'You want me or not, Bass? I'm gonna count to five. One, two, three, four . . .'

'All right, all right, follow it up.'

'Fine, Jack. Now, a little matter. . . .'

'What?'

'I'll need a month in advance.'

'A month? I thought you were hot on it.'

'I gotta lay the trap. I gotta set it up. I gotta make sure. When he hits that gong . . .'

'All right, all right, the check is on the way!'

He slammed the phone down on me. Acted like a guy in love. What a sucker. . . .

Next I phoned Grovers. He had given me his business number. The phone rang 3 times, he picked it up.

'Hello,' he said, 'This is the Silver Haven Mortuary.'

'Jesus,' I said.

'What?' he asked.

'Grovers, you play with stiffs.'

'What?' he asked.

'Stiffs. Stiffs. This is Nick Belane.'

'What do you want, Mr. Belane?'

'I'm working on your space alien case, Mr. Grovers.'

'Yes, I remember.'

'Tell me, Hal, why do you do what you do?'

'What do you mean?'

'Playing with the dead. Why? Why?'

'It's my occupation. A man has to make a living.'

'But playing with stiffs? That's kind of weird. That's sick. Do you drain the blood? What do you do with the blood after you drain it?'

'I have an employee who does that, Billy French.'

'Put him on, I want to talk to him.'

'He's out to lunch.'

'You mean, he eats?'

'Yes.'

I paused. I inhaled, I exhaled. Then I spoke. 'Look, Grovers, you want me to follow up this case?'

'You mean, Jeannie Nitro?'

'Of course. You got any other space babes working?'

'No.'

'Well, you want me to get her off your neck?'

'Of course. But do you think you can? Looks to me like you struck out the only time you met her.'

'Grovers, even Ted Williams struck out now and then. I'll finally slam that whore so far you'll never see her again!'

'I don't think she's a whore, Mr. Belane.'

'Just a manner of speaking. No offense meant against the bimbo.'

'Do you think you can do anything about her?'

'Even as we are speaking, Grovers, I am working on a link, a tie-in.'

'Like what?'

'I can't tell you too much. But the fact that you play with stiffs and that she is a space alien, that's a tie-in, a link.'

'What do you mean, Mr. Belane?'

'I can't tell you too much. But I have been consulting with a specialist in these matters. He's got a book on the space aliens but he requested more background on you.'

'All right, what do you want to know?'

'Hold it. Before I put any more time on this case, I'll need another check. Two weeks in advance.'

'Do you think you can do something?'

'God damn it, I've just told you, I'm in full swing on this matter!'

'All right, Mr. Belane, I'll get a check in the mail today. Two weeks.'

'You're a wise man, Mr. Grovers.'

'Yes.'

'Oh, Mr. Belane, Billy French just came back from lunch. You want to talk to him?'

'No, but ask him what he had for lunch.'

'Just a moment . . .'

I waited. Then he was back. 'He said roast beef and mashed potatoes.'

'That's sickening!'

'What?'

'I've got to go now, Mr. Grovers.'

'But I thought you wanted more background on me.'

'I'll send you a questionnaire.'

I hung up, swung my feet up on the desk. I was putting the pieces back in line. I was there. Nick Belane, dick. Yet I still had to solve the Red Sparrow affair. And then there was Celine and Lady Death. There was always Lady Death.

Now there was a whore.

I mean, what else could you call her?

20

I had to think about it. I had to think about all of it. Somehow, it was all tying together: space, death, Sparrow, stiffs, Celine, Cindy, Bass. But I couldn't quite fit the pieces together. Not yet. My temples began to throb. I had to get out of there.

The office walls held no answers. I was going goofy, I began to think of myself in bed with Lady Death, Cindy and Jeannie Nitro, all of them, at once. All too much. I put on my derby and walked out the door.

I found myself at the racetrack. Hollywood Park. There were no live horses. They were at Oak Tree. The races were telecast and you bet as usual.

I took the escalator up. Guy behind me bumped against one of my hip pockets.

'Oh, sorry,' he said. 'Pardon me.'

I always carried my wallet in my left front pocket. You learned, you learned. After a while.

Passed the Turf Club. Looked in. Just a bunch of old guys. With money. How did they do it? And how much did you need? And what did it all mean? We all died broke and most of us lived that way. It was a debilitating game. Just to get your shoes on in the morning was a victory.

I pushed open the door and stepped into the clubhouse area. And there was the mailman standing there sucking on a coffee. I walked up to him.

'Who the hell let you in here?' I asked him.

His face looked out of shape. Swollen.

'Belane,' he said, 'I'm going to kill you.'

'You shouldn't drink coffee,' I said, 'it will keep you awake nights.'

'I'm going to take you out, Belane, your days are numbered.'

'Who do you like in the first?' I asked him.

'*Dog Ears.*'

'Here,' I handed him a couple of bucks, 'get lucky.'

'Hey, thanks Belane!'

'Forget it,' I said, then walked off.

Something was always after a man. It never relented. No rest, ever.

I walked over to concessions and got a large coffee.

'Who do you like in the first, Belane?' the waitress asked.

'Can't tell you or you'll beat the odds down to nothing.'

'Thanks, jerk,' she said.

I slid her tip back across the counter and put it back in my pocket. I found a seat near the screen and sat down and opened the *Form*. Then I heard a voice behind me.

'That two bucks ain't gettin' you off, Belane. You're finished.'

It was the mailman. I stood up and turned around.

'Give me the two fucking bucks back then!'

'No way, man!'

'I'll bust your damned sack!' I told him.

He smiled and moved toward me. I felt the edge of the blade pressed against my gut. It was just the tip, he had the rest covered with his fingers.

'I got 6 inches here and I'd just love to sink it into your stupid, fat gut!'

'How come you're not working today? Who the hell's delivering the mail?'

'Shut up! I'm trying to decide whether to kill you or not.'

'Buddy, I got 10 bucks here for you to bet on *Dog Ears*.'

'How much?'

'$20.'

'How much?'

I felt the tip of the knife prick my skin.

'$50.'

'All right, reach into your wallet, slip out a $50 and stick it in my front shirt pocket.'

I felt the sweat rolling down behind my ears. I worked the wallet out of my left front pocket, slipped out a $50 and slipped it into his front pocket. I felt the tip of the knife withdraw.

'Now, sit down there and open up your *Form* and begin reading it.'

I did that. Then I felt the tip of the knife against the back of my neck.

'Feel lucky,' he said.

Then he walked off.

I sat there and finished my coffee. Then I got up and walked out. I took the escalator down, got to parking, got into my car and drove out of there. Some days just weren't your days. I drove all the way to Hollywood, parked it somewhere and walked into a movie. I got some popcorn and a soft drink and sat down. The movie was on but I didn't watch it. I just chewed at the popcorn and sucked at the drink. And wondered if *Dog Ears* had taken the first.

21

I couldn't sleep that night. I drank beer, I drank wine, I drank vodka, all to no avail.

I hadn't solved anything. All my cases were dormant. My father had told me that I would be a failure. He was a failure also. Bad seed.

I flipped on the TV. I had one in the bedroom. A young woman came on and told me that she would talk to me, make me feel good. All I needed was a credit card. I decided against it. Then the woman's face vanished from the screen and it was Jeannie Nitro's face.

'Belane,' she said, 'I don't want you messing in my affairs.'

'What?' I said.

She repeated the sentence and I switched the TV off. I poured another vodka, straight. I switched out the lights and sat in bed in the dark. I took a hit of the vodka.

Then there was a large buzzing sound like a cloud of bees circling a disturbed hive. Then there was a flash of purple light and Jeannie Nitro stood there. It scared the hell out of me.

'Scare you, Belane?' she asked.

'Hell no,' I answered, 'don't you have any manners? Don't you knock before you enter?'

Jeannie Nitro looked about the room.

'You need a maid,' she told me, 'this place is filthy.'

I drained my vodka, tossed the glass to one side.

'Never mind that, I'm going to nail your ass.'

'As a detective, you lack three things.'

'Like?'

'Drive, direction and detection.'

'Yeah? Well, I'm on to your game, baby.'

'Is that so?'

'You're sucking up to Grovers because he's a mortician and because you want to use his dead bodies to house your alien friends in.'

She sat down in a chair, found one of my cigarettes, lit it and laughed.

'Do I look like I'm in a dead body?'

'Not exactly.'

'We can create our own bodies. Watch!'

Again there was the buzzing sound, a flash of purple light and over in the corner of the room appeared another Jeannie Nitro. She was standing by my potted plant.

'Hello, Belane,' she said.

'Hello, Belane,' said the Jeannie Nitro sitting in the chair.

'Hey,' I said, 'can you be in two bodies at the same time?'

'No,' said the Jeannie Nitro sitting in the chair. 'But,' said the Jeannie Nitro standing by the potted plant, 'we can leap from one body to another.'

I climbed out of bed to pick up my glass and pour another vodka.

'You sleep in your shorts,' said one Jeannie Nitro.

'Disgusting,' said the other.

I got back into bed with my drink and propped myself up against a pillow.

There was another sound of buzzing, a flash of purple light and the Jeannie by the potted plant was gone. I looked at the one in the chair.

'Look,' I said, 'Grovers hired me to get you off his ass and that's just what I intend to do.'

'You talk big for a man whose talents hover near the zero mark.'

'Yeah? Well, I've cracked tougher cases than yours!'

'Really? Tell me about one of them.'

'All my back files are confidential.'

'Confidential or non-existent?'

'Don't get me pissed, Jeannie or I'll . . .'

'You'll what?'

'I'll . . .' I lifted the vodka toward my mouth. Suddenly my hand froze two inches from my lips. I couldn't move.

'You're 3rd rate, Belane. Don't play with me. And I'm being kind now. Feel lucky.'

Feel lucky? That was the second time I had heard that within 12 hours.

There was the buzz, the flash of purple and Jeannie Nitro was gone.

I sat there in bed, unable to move, the glass still two inches from my lips. I sat and waited. I had time to muse over my career. There wasn't much to muse about. Maybe I was in the wrong profession. But it was too late to start anything else.

I just sat there and waited. In about ten minutes there was a tingling all over my body. I was able to move my hand just a little. Then a little more. I put the vodka to my lips, managed to tilt my head and I drained the glass. I tossed it to the floor, stretched out in bed and waited once more for sleep. I heard the sound of gunfire outside and realized that everything was all right with the world. In five minutes I was asleep along with everybody else.

22

I awakened depressed. I looked up at the ceiling, at the cracks in the ceiling. I saw a buffalo running over something. I think it was me. Then I saw a snake with a rabbit in his mouth. The sun came through the rips in the shade and formed a swastika on my belly. My bunghole itched. Were my hemorrhoids coming back? My neck was stiff and my mouth tasted like sour milk.

I got up and walked to the bathroom. I hated to look in that mirror but I did. And I saw depression and defeat. Sagging dark pouches under the eyes. Little cowardly eyes, the eyes of a rodent trapped by the frigging cat. My flesh looked like it wasn't trying. It looked like it hated being part of me. My eyebrows hung down, twisted, they looked as if they were demented, demented eyebrow hairs. Horrible. I looked disgusting. And I wasn't even ready for a bowel movement. I was all plugged up. I walked over to the toilet to piss. I aimed properly but somehow it came out sideways and splashed on the floor. I tried to re-aim and pissed all over the toilet seat which I had forgotten to lift. I ripped off some toilet paper and mopped up. Cleaned the seat. Tossed the paper into the can and flushed. I walked to the window and looked out and saw a cat shit on the roof next door. Then I turned back, found my toothbrush, squeezed the tube. Too much came out. It flopped wearily against my brush and fell into the sink. It was green. It was like a green worm. I stuck my finger into it, stuck some of it on the brush and began brushing. Teeth. What god-damned things they were. We had to eat. And eat and eat again. We were all disgusting, doomed to our dirty little tasks. Eating and farting and scratching and smiling and celebrating holidays.

I finished brushing my teeth and went back to bed. I had no kick left, no zing. I was a thumbtack, I was a piece of linoleum.

I decided to stay in bed until noon. Maybe by then half the world would be dead and it would only be half as hard to take. Maybe if I got up at noon I'd look better, feel better. I knew a guy once who didn't excrete for days. He finally just exploded. Really. Shit flew out of his belly.

Then the phone rang. I let it ring. I never answered the phone in the morning. It rang 5 times and stopped. There. I was alone with myself. And disgusting as I was it was better than being with somebody else, anybody else, all of them out there doing their pitiful little tricks and handsprings. I pulled the covers up to my neck and waited.

23

I got to the track for the 4th race. I had to break through somewhere. All my leads were stalled. I pulled out the list. I had it all written down:

1. Find out if Celine *is* Celine. Inform Lady Death of findings.
2. Locate the Red Sparrow.
3. Find out if Cindy is screwing around on Bass. If so, nail her ass.
4. Get the Space Alien off of Grovers' back.

I folded the list and put it back in my pocket. I opened the *Form*. They were coming out on the track for the 4th. It was a warm easy day. Everything seemed in a dream state. Then I heard a sound behind me. There was somebody sitting behind me. I turned. It was Celine. He smiled at me.

'Nice day,' he said.

'What the hell you doing here?' I asked him.

'Paid my way in. They didn't ask any questions,' said Celine.

'You tailing me, motherfucker?' I asked.

'I was going to ask you the same thing,' he said.

'There are a lot of things I don't understand,' I told him.

'Me neither,' he said. Then he climbed over the seat and sat down next to me. 'We're going to talk,' he said.

'Sure,' I said, 'now, first off, what's your name? Your real name?'

I felt the snub-nosed revolver poking me in the side. He was holding it under his coat.

'You got a permit for that thing?' I asked.

'I'll ask the questions here,' he said, giving me a little poke with the firearm.

'Go ahead,' I said.

'Who put the tail on me?'

'Lady Death.'

'Lady Death?' he laughed. 'Don't give me that crap!'

'I crap you not. That's what she calls herself, "Lady Death."'

'Some nut, huh?'

'Maybe.'

'Where can I find this bitch?'

'I don't know. She only contacts me.'

'You expect me to buy that?'

'I don't know, it's all I got to sell.'

'What's she want?'

'She wants to know if you're the real Celine.'

'Yeah?'

'Yeah.'

'Who do you like in this race?' he asked.

'*Green Moon*,' I told him.

'*Green Moon*? That's my selection.'

'OK,' I said, 'let me go bet. I'll be right back.'

I started to rise.

'Sit down,' he intoned, 'before I blow your balls off.'

I sat down.

'Now,' he said, 'I want this woman off my tail. Also, I want her real name. I'm not buying this Lady Death thing. And I want you to get busy on this matter. In fact, beginning now!'

'But *she's* my client. How can you be my client?'

'You figure it out, fat boy.'

'Fat boy?'

'You got stuff hanging from your gut.'

'Hanging or not hanging, if I work for you I get paid, and I don't come cheap.'

'Name it.'

'6 bucks an hour.'

He reached into his pocket and came out with a roll of bills. He dropped them down my shirt front.

'Here's a month in advance.'

Then there was a roar from the crowd. They were coming down the stretch and who was leading by 3? And who won by 4? *Green Moon*. Odds: 6 to 1.

'Shit,' I told him, 'you cost me a score. *Green Moon* got it all.'

'Shut up,' he said, 'and get busy on my case.'

'All right, all right,' I said, 'where do I contact you?'

'Here's my number,' he said, handing me a tiny piece of paper.

Then he got up, walked down the aisle and was gone.

I knew I was in the middle of something big but I

couldn't unscramble it. Well, I had to get busy, that's all.

I opened the *Form* and checked out the 5th race.

24

The next day I went down to the Silver Haven Mortuary to check things out there. Damn good business to get into – no slack periods. I parked outside and went in. Nice place. Hushed hall. Thick, dirty rugs. I walked around and into another large room. It was full of caskets. Big ones, little ones, fat ones, thin ones. Some people purchased their caskets ahead of time. Not me. To hell with it.

There didn't seem to be anybody about. I could boost a casket. I could rope it to my car. Drive away. Where was Grovers? Where was anybody?

Then I got a little itch and the itch got worse. And then I did it. I lifted a casket lid and looked inside. I SCREAMED. And slammed the lid.

There had been a naked woman in there. Young, a looker, but dead. Wow!

Hal Grovers came running in.

'BELANE! WHAT ARE YOU DOING?'

'DOING? DOING? WHAT DO YOU MEAN? WHERE THE HELL *YOU* BEEN, GROVERS?'

'THE MEN'S ROOM. WHAT WERE YOU SCREAMING ABOUT?'
I pointed.

'YOU GOT A STIFF IN THAT CASKET! A BABE! BIG JUGS!'
Grovers walked over and opened the lid.

'There isn't a body in here, Mr. Belane.'

'What?'

I walked over and looked. The coffin was empty.

I whirled and grabbed Grovers by the lapels.

'Don't play games with me, baby! I saw it! I saw her *box*! A young dead bimbo! You playing games with me? You and . . . Billy French . . . the blood-sucker! I'm not a man to play with, Grovers!'

'Nobody is playing with you, Belane. You're hallucinating.'

I let go of his lapels.

'Sorry,' I said, 'I should have known.'

'Known what?'

'It's Jeannie Nitro. She's playing with my mind. She knows I'm on your case.'

'I haven't seen her lately. Maybe she's gone.'

'She's not gone. She's waiting, Grovers.'

'Waiting for what?'

'I don't know right now.'

I spun on my heel and looked all around.

'Grovers, quick! How many dead do you have here now?'

'We've prepared two. They are in the Slumber Room.'

'I've got to see them!'

'What?'

'You want me to crack this case or not?'

'I want you to . . . crack it.'

'Then I'll have to look at the two stiffs.'

'Why?'

'If I told you, you'd never guess.'

'What does that mean?'

'Never mind. Now let me have a look.'

'This is highly irregular.'

'Come on! Come on!'

'Very well. Follow me . . .'

We went into the Slumber Room. Classy place. Dark. Candles burning. There were three caskets.

'OK, lemme see,' I told Grovers.

'Could you please tell me why?'

'Jeannie Nitro wants to house her space aliens in these dead bodies. Give them a shell, a hiding place. A shell, you know, like a turtle. Nitro is hanging around you to get at these bodies.'

'But these are dead bodies, they are in a state of decay. Besides, we are going to bury them. How can they use them?'

'The space aliens hide in the dead bodies until they are buried, then they find other dead bodies.'

'But if they want to hide, why would they use dead bodies? Why wouldn't they hide in storage tanks or caves or something like that? Why wouldn't they use live bodies?'

'You fool, the live bodies would react to their presence. Open these caskets, Grovers! I think they are in there now!'

'Belane, I think you're mad!'

'Go on, open them!'

Grovers opened the first one. Nice oak casket. There was a fellow in there about 38, bushy red hair, dressed in a cheap suit.

I turned and looked at Grovers.

'One of them is in him now.'

'How do you know?'

'I just saw him move!'

'What?'

'I saw him move!'

I reached over and grabbed the man by the neck.

'Come on, come on! Get out of there! I know that you're in there!'

As I shook the head, the mouth opened a bit and spit out some white cotton.

I jumped back.

'SHIT! WHAT WAS THAT?'

Grovers let out a low moan.

'Belane, I worked for a good hour, padding his cheeks, making him look fulsome and healthy! Now he's all sagged in again! Now I've got to do it all over.'

'Sorry, I didn't realize. But I think we're closing in. Open another casket! Please!'

'You open it. This is truly disgusting. I don't know why I'm allowing this. I must be crazy.'

I walked over and opened a pine casket. I looked. And I kept looking. I couldn't believe it.

'Is this some kind of joke, Grovers? One doesn't joke in this fashion. It's not funny at all.'

The figure stretched out in the casket was me. The casket was lined in velvet and I was smiling a waxy smile. I was wearing a dark brown wrinkled suit and my hands were crossed over my chest and holding a white carnation.

I turned around and faced Grovers.

'What the hell's going on here, baby? Where'd you get this one?'

'Oh, that's Mr. Andrew Douglas, died suddenly of a heart attack. Been a community leader here for some decades.'

'That's crap, Grovers. That stiff in there is me! *Me!*'

'Nonsense,' said Grovers. He walked over and looked into the coffin.

'It's Mr. Douglas.'

I walked over and looked in. It was some old white-haired guy, 70 or 80 years old. He looked pretty good, they had rouged his cheeks and put on just a touch of lipstick. His skin glowed as if they had waxed it. But it wasn't me.

'It's Jeannie Nitro,' I said, 'she's fucking with us.'

'I think you are a very confused man, Mr. Belane.'

'Shut up,' I said.

I had to think. Somewhere it all fit. It had to fit.

Just then another man entered and stood in the doorway.

'The body has been prepared, Hal.'

'Thank you, Billy. You can leave.'

Billy French turned and walked out.

'Jesus, Grovers, doesn't he wash his hands?'

'What do you mean?'

'I saw red on his hands.'

'Nonsense.'

'I saw red.'

'Mr. Belane, would you care to look into the third coffin? Although it's empty. A gentleman has selected it in advance.'

I turned around and stared at it.

'Is he *in* there, Grovers?'

'No, the gentleman is still alive. It's a pre-select. We

give ten percent off on pre-selects. Would you care for one? We have a lovely selection.'

'Thanks, Grovers, but I have an appointment some-where . . . I'll contact you.'

I spun on my heel and walked out the doorway, down the hall and out into the good, clean air. Any son-of-a-bitch who picks out his own casket is the same son-of-a-bitch who diddles with himself 6 times a week.

I got into my Bug, kicked it over and sliced out into traffic. Some guy in a van thought I had cut him off. He gave me the finger. I gave him the finger back.

It was beginning to rain. I rolled up the good window on the right hand side and snapped on the radio.

25

I took the elevator up to the 6th floor. The psychiatrist's name was Seymour Dundee. I pushed the door open and the waiting room was packed with nuts. One guy was reading a newspaper and holding it upside-down. Most of the others, men and women, sat silently. They didn't even appear to be breathing. There was a heavy dark feel to the room. I signed in at the desk and took my seat. Guy next to me was wearing one brown shoe and one black. 'Hey, buddy,' he said.

'Yeah,' I answered.

'Got change for a penny?' he asked.

'No,' I told him, 'not today.'

'Tomorrow maybe?' he went on.

'Maybe tomorrow,' I said.

'But maybe I won't be able to find you tomorrow,' he complained.

I hope not, I thought.

We waited and waited. All of us. Didn't the shrink know that waiting was one of the things that drove people crazy? People waited all their lives. They waited to live, they waited to die. They waited in line to buy toilet paper. They waited in line for money. And if they didn't have any money they waited in longer lines. You waited to go to sleep and then you waited to awaken. You waited to get married and you waited to get divorced. You waited for it to rain, you waited for it to stop. You waited to eat and then you waited to eat again. You waited in a shrink's office with a bunch of psychos and you wondered if you were one.

I must have waited for so long that I slept and I must have been awakened by the receptionist shaking me, 'Mr. Belane, Mr. Belane, you're next!'

She was an ugly old gal, she was uglier than I was. She startled me, her face was very close to mine. That's what death must be like, I thought, like this old gal.

'Honey,' I said, 'I'm ready.'

'Follow me,' she said.

I went through the office and followed her up the aisle. She opened a door and here sat this very satisfied looking guy behind his desk, dark green shirt, unbuttoned floppy orange sweater. Dark shades, smoking a cigarette in a holder.

'Sit down,' he motioned to a chair.

The receptionist closed the door and was off somewhere.

Dundee began doodling on a piece of paper with his pen. Looking down at the paper he said, 'This is costing you $160 an hour.'

'Screw you,' I said.

He looked up. 'Ha! I like that!'

He doodled some more, then said, 'Why are you here?'

'I don't know where to begin.'

'Begin by counting to ten backwards.'

'Screw your mother,' I told him.

'Ha!' said Dundee, 'have you had intercourse with yours?'

'What kind? Vocal? Spiritual? Clarify.'

'You know what I mean.'

'No, I don't.'

He made a round hole with the thumb and forefinger of his left hand, then ran the index finger of his right hand in and out of the hole. 'Like this,' he said, 'hmmm . . .'

'Yeah,' I said, 'I remember, she held her hand up like that once and I did it like that with my finger.'

'Are you here to mock me?' said Dundee. 'Do not make fun of me!'

I leaned over the desk toward him, 'You're lucky, buddy, that you're only getting mocked!'

'Oh,' he leaned back in his chair, 'is that so?'

'Yeah. Don't toy with me, baby, I am not to be held responsible.'

'Please, please, Mr. Belane, what is it you want?'

I slammed my fist down in the center of his desk. 'GOD DAMN IT, I NEED HELP!'

'Of course, Mr. Belane, where did you find me?'

'Yellow pages.'

'Yellow pages? I'm not in the yellow pages.'

'Yes, you are. Seymour Dundee, psychiatrist, Garner Building, room 604.'

'This is room 605. I'm Samuel Dillon, lawyer. Mr. Dundee is next door. I'm afraid you've made a mistake.'

I stood up and smiled. 'You're playing with me now, Dundee, you're trying to get even! If you think you can outmaneuver me, you've got chicken shit for brains!'

I was there to find out if the matter of Celine, the Red Sparrow, Lady Death, Space Aliens, Sam and Cindy Bass was really real or if I was actually having mental problems. I mean, none of it really made sense. Was I out of it? And where was I going with it and why?

The guy who called himself Samuel Dillon pushed a buzzer on his desk and soon the receptionist was back. She was still uglier than I. Nothing had changed.

'Molly,' he said, 'please escort this gentleman next door to Dr. Dundee's office. Thank you.'

I followed her along and out into the hall where she opened door #604 and whispered to me, 'Get straight, jerkoff . . .'

I walked into another packed waiting room. First thing I saw was the fellow with one brown shoe and one black shoe who had asked me for change for a penny. He saw me.

'Hey, Mr. . . .' he said.

I walked over to him. 'Happened to you too, huh?' he asked.

'What?'

'He he . . . got the wrong door . . . got the wrong door . . .'

I turned around then and walked out of there, took the elevator down. Then I waited for it to reach the first floor. Then I waited for the door to open. Then I walked down the hall and out onto the street and found my car. I got in. Started up. Waited for it to get warm. Got to a signal. It was red. I waited. I pushed in the cigarette lighter and waited. The light turned green, the lighter jumped out and I lit my smoke while driving along. I felt like I had better get over to the office. I felt like somebody was waiting for me.

26

I was wrong. There was nobody at the office. I went around and sat behind my desk.

I was feeling peculiar. So many things didn't fit. I mean, in the lawyer's office, why was that man reading his newspaper upside-down? He belonged in the shrink's office. Or maybe just the outside pages of the newspaper were upside-down and he was reading the inside straight-side-up? Was there a God? And where was the Red Sparrow? I had too many things to solve. Getting out of bed in the morning was the same as facing the blank wall of the Universe. Maybe I should go to a nude bar and stick a 5 buck bill into a G-string? Try to forget everything. Maybe I should go to a boxing match and watch two guys beat the shit out of each other?

But trouble and pain were what kept a man alive. Or trying to avoid trouble and pain. It was a full time job. And sometimes even in sleep you couldn't rest. Last dream I had I was laying under this elephant, I couldn't move and he was releasing one of the biggest turds you ever saw, it was about to drop and then my cat, Hamburger, walked across the top of my head and I awakened. You tell that dream to a shrink and he'll make something awful out of it. Because you are paying him excessively, he's going to make sure to make you feel bad. He'll tell you that the turd is a penis and that you are either frightened of it or that you want it, some kind of crap like that. What he really means is that *he* is frightened or wants the penis. It's only a dream about a big elephant turd, nothing more. Sometimes things are just what they seem to be and that's all there is to it. The best interpreter of the dream is the dreamer. Keep your money in your pocket. Or bet it on a good horse.

I had a hit of *sake*, cold. My ears jumped and I felt a little better. I could feel my brain beginning to warm up. I wasn't dead yet, just in a state of rapid decay. Who wasn't? We were all in the same leaky boat, jollying ourselves up. Like, you take Christmas. Yeah, take it the hell out of here. The man who made it up was the man who never carried extra luggage. The rest of us have got to dump most of our junk just to find out where we are. Well, not where we are but where we aren't. The more stuff you dumped the more you could see. Everything worked in reverse. Go backwards and Nirvana leaps into your lap. Sure.

I had another hit of *sake*. I was coming around.

Around the bend. Balls away. I was Nick Belane, super dick.

Then the phone rang. I picked it up just like a normal person would pick up a telephone. Well, not quite. Sometimes a phone made me think of an elephant turd. You know, all the shit you hear. A phone is a phone but what comes through it is another matter.

'You're a lousy philosopher,' said Lady Death.

'For me,' I told her, 'I'm perfect.'

'People live on their delusions,' she said.

'Why not?' I suggested. 'What else is there?'

'The end of them,' she said.

'Well, hell,' I said.

'Hell yourself,' said Lady Death. 'What's happening with the Celine caper?'

'Baby, I've got it all worked out.'

'Clue me, fat boy.'

'I want you to meet me at Musso's tomorrow afternoon at 2:30.'

'All right. But you better have something. Do you?'

'Babe, I can't tip my hat.'

'What the hell do you mean by that?'

'Sorry. I mean, I can't tip my *hand*.'

'You better have something . . .'

'I'll bet my life on it,' I told her.

'You just did,' said Lady Death, hanging up.

I put the phone down, stared at it a while. I picked an old cigar out of the ashtray, lit it, gagged.

Then I picked up the phone and punched out Celine's number.

It rang four times. Then I heard his voice.

'Yeah?'

'Sir, you've won a 2 pound box of chocolate covered cherries and a free trip to Rome.'

'Whoever you are, don't fuck with me.'

'This is Nick Belane . . .'

'I'll take the chocolates . . .'

'I want you to meet me at Musso's tomorrow afternoon at 2:30.'

'Why?'

'Just show up, Frenchy, and your troubles will be over.'

'You buying?'

'Yes.'

'I'll be there . . .'

He hung up.

Nobody ever said goodbye anymore. Not in our world.

I stared at the *sake*.

Then went for it.

27

It was 2:15 p.m. I was holding down a table at Musso's. I had a vodka-7 in front of me. Celine and Lady Death were about to meet. Two of my clients. Business was good, it was just without direction. Guy in the booth across the way kept staring at me. Some people stared, you know, like cows. They didn't know that they were doing it. I took a hit of my vodka, put it down, looked up. Guy was still staring. I'll give him two minutes, I thought, then if he doesn't stop, I'm going to bust his sack.

I got up to a minute and 45 seconds and then the guy stood up and started walking toward my table. I checked my holster. It was there. Snug. The best hard-on a man could have. Guy looked like a parking lot attendant. Or maybe a dentist. He had an ugly mustache and a false smile. Or maybe it was a false mustache and an ugly smile. He got close to my table, stopped, loomed there.

'Look, buddy,' I said, 'I'm sorry, I don't have any loose change.'

'I'm not hittin' you for coin, baby,' he said.

He made me nervous. He had eyes like a dead fish.

'What's your ache, then?' I asked him. 'They throw you out of your motel room?'

'Naw,' he said, 'I live with my mother.'

'How old are you?'

'46,' he told me.

'That's sick.'

'No, *she* is. Incontinent. Rubber diapers. The whole bit.'

'Oh,' I said, 'I'm sorry.'

'Me too.'

He just loomed there.

'Well,' I said, 'I don't know what I can do about that.'

'You can't do nothing . . .'

I finished my drink.

'I just wanted to ask you,' he said, 'I just wanted to ask you something.'

'OK. OK. Do it.'

'Aren't you Spike Jenkins?'

'Who?'

'Spike Jenkins. You used to fight out of Detroit, heavyweight. I saw you fight Tiger Forster. One of the greatest fights I ever saw.'

'Who won?' I asked.

'Tiger Forster.'

'I'm not Jenkins. Go sit down back where you were.'

'You wouldn't shit me? You're not Spike Jenkins?'

'Never was.'

'Well, I'll be damned.'

He turned around, walked back to his booth and sat down again, just like I told him to.

I looked at my watch. It was right on 2:30. Where were they?

I signaled the waiter for another drink . . .

At 2:35 Celine walked in. He stood there a moment, looking about. I waved my napkin on a fork. He walked over, sat down.

'I'll have a scotch and soda,' he said. His timing was good. The waiter was just arriving with my 2nd drink. I gave the waiter the order.

I drank my drink right off. I was feeling odd. Like nothing mattered, you know. Lady Death. Death. Or Celine. The game had worn me down. I'd lost my kick. Existence was not only absurd, it was plain hard work. Think of how many times you put on your underwear in a lifetime. It was appalling, it was disgusting, it was stupid.

Then the guy from the booth was looming there again. He looked at Celine.

'Hey, ain't this guy here with you, ain't he Spike Jenkins?'

'Sir,' Celine looked at him, 'if you value your balls in their present shape, please go away quickly.'

The guy left again.

'All right,' said Celine, 'why am I here?'

'I am going to bring you into contact with Lady Death.'

'So, death is a lady, eh?'

'Sometimes . . .'

Celine's drink arrived. He poured it right down.

'This Lady Death,' he asked, 'are we going to expose her?'

'You ever see Spike Jenkins fight?'

'No.'

'He looked like me,' I told him.

'That doesn't seem to be much of an accomplishment.'

Then *she* walked in. Lady Death. She was dressed to kill. She walked over to our table, put it down on the chair.

'Whiskey sour,' she said.

I nodded the waiter over. Gave him the order.

'I really don't know how to introduce you two because I'm not sure who either of you are,' I told him.

'What kind of dick are you?' Celine asked.

'The best in LA.'

'Yes? What's LA stand for?'

'Lost Assholes.'

'You been drinking?'

'Recently,' I answered.

Lady Death's whiskey sour arrived. She slammed it down. Then looked at Celine.

'So, introduce yourself. What's your name?'

'Spike Jenkins.'

'Spike Jenkins is dead.'

'How do you know?'

'I know.'

I nodded the waiter over and ordered 3 more drinks.

Then we just sat and looked at each other.

'Now,' I said, 'what we have here is a stalemate, a definite stalemate. Meanwhile, I'm buying all the drinks. So, let's make a little bet and the one who loses buys the next round.'

'What kinda bet?' asked Celine.

'Oh, something simple, like how many numbers on your driver's license. I mean the numbers which indicate the license itself.'

'Sounds stupid,' said Celine.

'Be a sport,' I said.

'Don't be chicken,' said Lady Death.

'Well, I'll have to guess,' said Celine.

'Take a shot,' I said.

'Give it your best, baby,' said Lady Death.

'OK,' said Celine, 'I'll say 8.'

'I'll take 7,' said Lady Death.

'I'll take 5,' I said.

'Now,' I said, 'let's look at our licenses, let's have a look.'

We dug them out.

'Ah,' said Lady Death, 'mine has 7!'

'Damn it,' I said, 'mine has 7.'

'Mine has 8,' said Celine.

'That can't be,' I said, 'here, let me have a look.'

I reached out and took his license. I counted.

'Yours has 7. You counted the letter which precedes the numbers. That's what you did. Here, look . . .'

I handed the license to Lady Death. There were 7 numbers and also some other information: LOUIS FERDINAND DESTOUCHES, b. 1894–.

God damn. I began to tremble all over. Not large trembles but good sized ones. With great will power I brought them down to a rather continuous shiver. All too much. It was *him*, sitting there with us at a table in Musso's in an afternoon which was leaning toward the 21st century.

Lady Death was ecstatic, that's all, ecstatic. She looked truly beautiful, glowing all over.

'Gimme my god-damned driver's license,' said Celine.

'Sure, big boy,' said Lady Death, smiling, handing it back.

'Well,' I said to Celine, 'looks like both you and I lost. So we'll flip a coin to decide who buys, OK?'

'Sure,' said Celine.

I got out my lucky quarter, flipped it up in the air and yelled at Celine: 'Call it!'

'Tails!' he yelled.

It hit the table and sat there. Heads.

I picked up the quarter and put it back into my pocket. 'Somehow,' I said to Celine, 'I have a feeling that this isn't going to be your day.'

'It's going to be my day,' said Lady Death.

And like that, the drinks arrived.

'Put these on my tab,' Celine told the waiter.

We sat there with our drinks.

'Somehow I feel like I've been taken,' said Celine.

He slugged his drink down.

'They warned me about you LA creeps.'

'You still practice medicine?' I asked him.

'I'm gettin' out of here,' he said.

'Ah, come on,' said Lady Death, 'have another drink. Life is short.'

'No, I'm gettin' the hell out of here!'

He tossed a 20 on the table, got up and walked toward the exit, then was gone.

'Well,' I said to Lady Death, 'he's gone . . .'

'Not quite,' she said.

There was a sound, the sound of screeching brakes. There was a loud thump, like metal hitting flesh. I jumped up from the table and ran outside. There in the middle of Hollywood Boulevard was the still body of Celine. A fat woman in a big red hat, who had been driving the ancient Olds, got out and screamed and screamed and screamed. Celine was very still. I knew that he was dead.

I turned around and walked back into Musso's. Lady D. was gone. I sat back down at the table. My drink was untouched. I took care of that. Then I just sat there. The good die old, I thought. Then I just sat there some more.

'Hey, Jenkins,' I heard a voice, 'all your friends are gone. Where'd all your friends go?'

It was the Loomer. He was still there.

'What're you drinking?' I asked.

'Rum and coke.'

I got the waiter. 'Two rum and cokes,' I said, 'one for me and,' I pointed, 'one for him.'

The drinks arrived. The Loomer sat with his in his booth and I sat with mine at my table.

I heard the siren then. It's when you don't hear it, it's for you.

I drank my drink, got my tab, paid with my card, tipped 20% and got out of there.

28

The next day at the office I put my feet up on my desk and lit a good cigar. I considered myself a success. I had solved a case. I had lost two clients but I had solved a case. But the slate wasn't clean. There was still the Red Sparrow. And the Jack Bass matter with Cindy. And there was still Hal Grovers and that space alien, Jeannie Nitro. My thoughts jumped between Cindy Bass and Jeannie Nitro. It was pleasant thinking. Anyhow, it beat sitting in a duck blind waiting for them to fly over.

I got to thinking about solutions in life. People who solved things usually had lots of persistence and some good luck. If you persisted long enough, the good luck usually came. Most people couldn't wait on the luck, though, so they quit. Not Belane. No candyass, he. Top flight. Game. A bit lazy, perhaps. But crafty.

I pulled open the top right hand drawer, found the vodka and allowed myself a hit. A drink to victory. The winner writes the history books, is surrounded by the lovely virgins . . .

The phone rang. I picked it up. 'Belane, here.'

'You haven't seen the last of me,' the Lady said. It was Lady Death.

'Look, baby, can't we cut a deal?'

'It's never been done, Belane.'

'Let's break precedent, let's give it a shot, Lady.'

'No dice, Belane.'

'Well, OK, but how about giving me a date, you know, a D.O.D.?'

'What's that?'

'Date of Demise.'

'What good would that do?'

'Lady, I could prepare myself.'

'Every human should anyhow, Belane.'

'Lady, they don't, they forget it, they ignore it or they're just too stupid to think about it.'

'That doesn't concern me, Belane.'

'What concerns you, Lady?'

'My job.'

'Me too, Lady, my job concerns me.'

'Well, good for you, fat boy. This call was just to let you know that I haven't forgotten you . . .'

'Ah, thanks so much, Lady, you've really cheered up my day.'

'See you later, Belane . . .'

She hung up.

There's always somebody about to ruin your day, if not your life. I put out my cigar, put on my derby, went to the door, locked it, walked to the elevator and took it down. Out on the street I just stood there watching them walk around. My gut began to turn and I walked half a block down to a bar, The Eclipse, walked in, took a stool. I had to think. I had cases to solve and I didn't know where to begin. I ordered a whiskey sour with beer chaser. Actually, I felt like laying down somewhere and sleeping for a couple of weeks. The game was getting to me. At one time there had been some excitement. Not much, but some. You don't want to hear it. Married three times, divorced three times. Born and ready to die. Nothing to do but try to solve cases nobody else would touch. Not for my fee.

Guy at the end of the bar kept looking at me. I could feel him looking. The place was empty except for me, him, the barkeep. I finished my drink and called the bartender over for another. All he had was a lot of hair on his face.

'Same thing, huh?' he asked.

'Yeah,' I said, 'only stronger.'

'For the same price?' he asked.

'Whatever is possible,' I answered.

'What's that mean?'

'You don't know, barkeep?'

'Naw . . .'

'Well, while you're making my drink, think about it.'

He walked off.

The guy at the end caught my eye, waved, yelled, 'How ya doin', Eddie?'

'I'm not Eddie,' I told him.

'You look like Eddie,' he said.

'I don't give a fuck if I look like Eddie or not,' I answered.

'You lookin' for trouble?' he asked.

'Yeah,' I said, 'you gonna bring it?'

The barkeep brought my drink, took some of the

money I'd left on the bar, said, 'I don't think you're a nice man.'

'Who told you you could think?' I asked.

'I don't have to serve you,' he said.

'You don't want the money, I'll keep it.'

'I don't want it *that* bad. . . .'

'How bad do you want it, tell me . . .'

'DON'T SERVE HIM NO MORE!' yelled the guy at the end of the bar.

'One more word out of you and I'm gonna stick my foot up your ass! They'll be sucking red bubbles out of your cheeks with a rubber tube.'

The guy just smiled a weak smile. The bartender was still standing there.

'Look,' I said to him, 'I just walked in here for a quiet, peaceful drink and everybody starts to give me a lot of crap! By the way, have you seen the Red Sparrow?'

'The Red Sparrow? What's that?'

'You'll know it when you see it. Hell, never mind . . .'

I finished my drink and got out of there. It was better on the street. I just walked along. Something had to give and it wasn't going to be me. I began counting each fool that passed me. I got up to 50 in two-and-one-half-minutes, then stepped into the next bar.

29

I walked in and took a stool. The barkeep walked up.

'Hi, Eddie,' he said.

'I'm not Eddie,' I told him.

'I'm Eddie,' he said.

'You don't want to play with me,' I told him.

'No, you do it,' he said.

'Look, barkeep, I'm a peaceful man. Fairly normal. I don't sniff armpits or wear ladies' underwear. But everywhere I go, somebody is pushing shots at me, they give me no rest. Why is this?'

'I think you got it comin', somehow.'

'Well, Eddie, you stop thinking and see if you can fix me a double vodka and tonic, touch of lime.'

'We don't got no lime.'

'Yeah, you have. I can see it from here.'

'That lime's not for you.'

'Yeah? Who's it for? Elizabeth Taylor? Now, if you want to sleep in your own bed tonight, I'll have that lime. In my drink. Pronto.'

'Yeah? What ya gonna do? You and whose army?'

'One more word out of you, boy, and you're gonna have a breathing problem.'

He stood there looking at me, deciding whether to call my card or not. He blinked, then sensibly moved off and began working on my drink. I watched him carefully. No tricks. He brought the drink back.

'I was kidding, mister, can't you take a joke?'

'Depends upon how it's told.'

Eddie walked off again, stood down at the far end of the bar.

I lifted the drink, slammed it down. Then I pulled out a bill. I took the lime, squeezed it onto the bill. Then I rolled the bill around it, then rolled it down the bar toward the barkeep. It stopped in front of him. He looked down at it. I slowly stood up, did a little neck exercise, turned and walked out. I decided to go back to the office. I had work to do. My eyes were blue and nobody loved me but myself. I walked along humming my favorite bit from 'Carmen.'

30

I unlocked the door to my office, swung it open, and there she was: Jeannie Nitro, sitting on my desk, legs crossed, kicking her heels.

'Belane, you pitiful drunk, how ya doing?' she smiled.

She looked great. I could see where Grovers was in trouble. What did it matter if she was a space alien? The way she looked you wanted more of them around. But

Grovers was my client. I had to do this one in, off her, move her out of the picture. I never got any rest. I was always on the hustle for somebody.

I swung around my desk, flopped on my chair, tossed my derby onto the hat rack, lit a cigar and sighed. Jeannie just sat on the desk, kicking her legs.

'To answer your question, Jeannie, I'm doin' all right.'

'I've come to make a deal with you, Belane.'

'I'd rather hear a Scarlatti sonata.'

'How long since you had a woman?'

'Who cares?'

'You should.'

'Suppose I don't?'

'Suppose you do?'

'You offering me your bod, Jeannie?'

'Maybe.'

'What's the maybe? Either you do or you don't.'

'The bod is part of the deal.'

'Which is?'

Jeannie popped off the desk and began walking the rug. She looked good walking the rug.

'Belane,' she said while still walking, 'I'm the first wave of an invasion force from Space. We are going to take over the earth.'

'Why?'

'I'm from the planet Zaros. We are overpopulated. We need the earth for our excess people.'

'Well, why in the hell don't you come on in? You look just like humans. Nobody would ever know.'

Jeannie stopped walking and faced me.

'Belane, we don't look like this. What you are seeing is only a mirage.'

Jeannie came over and sat down on my desk again.

'What do you really look like?' I asked.

'This,' she said.

There was a flash of purple light. I looked down on my desk. There was this *thing*. It looked like an above average size snake, only it was covered with coarse hair and at its center was a round, moist glob with a single eye. The head had no eyes, only a thin mouth. It was truly a hideous looking thing. I grabbed the telephone, raised it high and brought it down hard. I missed. The thing had slithered to one side. It crawled down along the rug. I ran after it to crush it with my shoe. There was another flash of purple light and then Jeannie stood there again.

'You fool,' she said, 'you tried to kill me. Don't anger me or I'll take you out!'

Her eyes were blazing.

'OK, baby, OK, I just got kind of confused. Sorry.'

'All right, forget it. Now, we are an advance force sent to scout the earth for our excess population. But we feel it would only be sensible to align some of you humans to our Cause. Like you.'

'Why me?'

'You're the perfect type, you're gullible, self-centered and have no character.'

'What's with Grovers? Why him? Why the dead bodies? How does he fit?'

Jeannie laughed.

'He doesn't. We just *landed* there. I became somewhat attached to him, just a mild flirtation, something to do. . . .'

'And me? You got the hots for me, baby?'

'You're usable for the Cause.'

She moved toward me. I was totally entranced. Her body was against mine, we pressed together. We embraced and our mouths joined. Her tongue darted into my mouth, it was hot and wiggled like a small snake.

I pushed her away.

'No,' I said, 'I'm sorry, I can't!'

She looked at me.

'What is it, Belane? You too old?'

'It's not that, baby . . .'

'What is it?'

'I don't want to hurt your feelings . . .'

'Tell me, Belane . . .'

'Well, you might turn into that ugly thing again with the bump in the middle and that one eye . . .'

'Why you fat fuck, Zaronians are beautiful!'

'I didn't think you'd understand . . .'

I walked back around my desk, sat down, pulled open the drawer, found the pint of vodka, unscrewed the cap, had a hit.

'How'd ya land?' I asked Jeannie.

'Space tube.'

'Space tube, huh? How many of you?'

'6.'

'I don't know if I can help you, baby . . .'

'You'll help me, Belane.'

'And if I don't?'

'You're dead.'

'Christ, first Lady Death. Now you. All you ladies do is threaten me with death. Well, maybe I'll have something to say about that!'

I reached into the drawer for the luger. I had it in my hand. I pulled off the safety catch and leveled the gat at her.

'I'll blow you all the way back to Zaros, baby!'

'Go ahead, pull the trigger!'

'What?'

'I said, pull the trigger, Belane!'

'You think I won't?'

I could already feel some sweat at my temples.

'You think I won't?' I repeated.

Jeannie just smiled at me.

'Pull the damned trigger, Belane!'

My whole face was a mass of sweat.

'Please go back to Zaros, sweetheart!'

'NO!'

I pulled the trigger. There was a roar of sound and the gun kicked back in my hand. I rubbed the sweat away from my eyes and looked.

Jeannie was standing there smiling at me. I looked closer. She had something in her mouth. It was the bullet. She had caught the bullet with her teeth. She walked toward the desk, stopped. Then she spat the bullet out into my ashtray.

'Baby,' I said, 'we can make a lot of money with that trick! We can team up! We can be rich! Think of it!'

'I wouldn't think of it, Belane. That would be a misuse of my powers.'

I took another hit of my vodka. I had a real problem here with Jeannie.

'Now,' said Jeannie, 'I am enlisting you for our Cause, the Cause of the Zaros, whether you like it or not. We are still revising our plan to inhabit the earth. You'll be contacted and advised at our discretion.'

'Look, Jeannie, can't you get anybody else for this god-damned thing?'

She smiled.

'Belane, you have been Selected!'

There was a flash of purple light and she was gone.

31

I got Grovers on the phone. He was in.

'How's business, Grovers?'

'Steady,' he said, 'no recession here.'

'Your case with Jeannie Nitro, it's closed. She won't be bothering you any more. I'll mail you a bill for final charges.'

'Final charges? You trying to stiff me?'

'Grovers, I got this alien babe off you. Now you pay up.'

'All right, all right . . . but how'd you do it?'

'Trade secret, baby.'

'All right, I suppose I should be grateful.'

'Don't suppose, just be. And pay your bill unless you want to be using one of your pine boxes. Or, do you prefer walnut?'

'Well, let's see . . .' he began.

I sighed and hung up.

I put my feet up on the desk. I was making progress. Now all I had to do was to nail Cindy Bass's ass and locate the Red Sparrow. Of course, Jeannie Nitro was now *my* problem. I was my own client. But Celine and Grovers were history. In a sense I was beginning to feel truly professional. But before I could relax, Lady Death entered my mind again. She was still there.

The phone rang, I picked it up. It was Lady Death.

'I'm still here, Belane.'

'Why don't you take a vacation, babe?'

'I can't. I enjoy my work too much.'

'Listen, can I ask you a question?'

'Sure.'

'Do you just work the earth?'

'What do you mean?'

'Well, I mean, does your work include, say, uh . . . space aliens?'

'Of course. Space aliens, worms, dogs, fleas, lions, spiders, you name it.'

'That's nice to know.'

'What's nice to know?'

'That you work space aliens.'

'You bore me, Belane.'

'I'm glad of that, baby.'

'Listen, I've got some work to do . . .'

'Just answer me one question . . .'

'Maybe. What is it?'

'How do you kill a space alien?'

'No problem.'

'A bullet won't do it. What do you use?'

'That's a secret of the trade, Belane.'

'You can tell me, baby, my lips will be forever sealed.'

'Fat boy,' she said just before hanging up, 'I might take care of that for you.'

I put the phone down and put my feet back on the desk. Christ, 6 space aliens on the prowl and enlisting me for the Cause. I should notify the authorities. Sure, lot of good that would do. I had to solve it myself. Seemed damned tough. Maybe I ought to sit on it for a while. I uncapped the vodka and had a little nip. After all, there was still the Red Sparrow and Cindy Bass. I took out a coin and flipped it: heads, Red Sparrow; tails, Cindy Bass. It came up tails. I smiled, leaned back in my chair and thought about her: Cindy Bass. Nailing it.

32

Well, to celebrate my progress as probably the greatest detective in LA I closed the office, took the elevator down and hit the street. I tried walking south, did, hit Sunset Boulevard and strolled along. Problem with Sunset, in my neighborhood, there weren't many bars. I walked along. Finally found one, half-a-class place. I didn't feel like sitting on a stool. I took a booth. Here came the waitress. She had on a mini-skirt, high heels, see-through blouse with padded brassiere. Everything was too small for her: her outfit, the world, her mind. Her face was hard as steel. When she smiled it hurt. It hurt her and it hurt me. She kept smiling. That smile was so false the hairs on my arms rose. I looked away.

'Hi, honey!' she said, 'watcha havin'?'

I didn't look at her face. I looked at her midriff. It was exposed. She had a little paper rose, red, pasted across her bellybutton. I talked to the paper rose.

'Vodka and tonic with lime.'

'Sure, honey!'

She minced off, trying to roll her buns attractively. It didn't work.

At once, I began to get depressed.

Don't, don't, Belane, I said to myself.

It didn't take. Everybody was screwed. There were no winners. There were only apparent winners. We were all chasing after a lot of nothing. Day after day. Survival seemed the only necessity. That didn't seem enough. Not with Lady Death waiting. It drove me crazy when I thought about it.

Don't think about it, Belane, I said to myself.

It didn't take.

The waitress arrived with my drink. I put down a bill. She picked it up.

'Thanks, honey!'

'Wait,' I said, 'bring me the change.'

'There isn't any change.'

'Then, consider your tip included.'

She opened her eyes large. They were blank.

'What're you, a god-damned cowboy?'

'What's a cowboy?'

'You don't know what a god-damned cowboy is?'

'No.'

'That's somebody who wants a free ride.'

'You think that up yourself?'

'No. That's what the girls call them.'

'What girls? The cowgirls?'

'Mister, you got a bug up your ass or what?'

'It's most probably "what." '

'MARY LOU!' I heard this loud voice, 'THAT ASSHOLE GIVING YOU TROUBLE?'

It was the bartender, a little guy with beetle brows.

'Don't worry, Andy, I'll handle this asshole.'

'Yeah, Mary Lou,' I said, 'you've probably handled a lot of assholes.'

'WHY YOU COCKSUCKER!' she screamed.

I saw Beetle Brows vaulting the bar. Good trick for a guy his size. I slammed my drink down and rose to meet him. I ducked under his right and dug my knee into his privates. He dropped, rolling on the floor. I kicked him in the ass and walked out onto Sunset Boulevard.

My luck in bars was getting worse and worse.

33

So I went to my place and drank and there went that day and that night.

I awakened about noon, eliminated some waste, brushed my teeth, shaved, mused. Didn't feel too bad. Didn't feel too much. I got dressed. I put on an egg, let it boil. I drank a glass of half-tomato and half-ale. I let the egg run under cold water, peeled it, ate it and then I was as ready as I would ever be.

I picked up the phone and got Jack Bass at his office. I told him who I was. He didn't seem happy with me.

'Jack,' I told him, 'remember that Frenchman I told you about?'

'Yeah? What about him?'

'I got him out of the way.'

'How?'

'He's dead.'

'Good. Was he the one?'

'Well, he was in contact with her.'

'Contact? What the hell you mean by that?'

'I don't want to hurt you.'

'Try me, Belane.'

'Listen, I'm trying to nail Cindy's ass. That's why you hired me. Right?'

'I don't know why I hired you. I think it was a mistake.'

'Jack, I got the Frenchman. He's dead.'

'So where do we stand?'

'He can't bang her.'

'Did he?'

'Jack . . .'

'Did you? All this "nail her ass" shit! Are you a pervert?'

'Look, I got a tight tail on Cindy. We want hard evidence.'

'There you go again!'

'We're closing in, Jack. It won't be long. Trust me.'

'Then there was more than the Frenchman?'

'I think so.'

'You think so? You think so? Hell, I'm paying you good money. It's been weeks and all you can tell me there's a dead Frenchman and "I think so"? You're just spinning your wheels! I want action! I want evidence! I want this thing busted wide open!'

'Within 7 days, Jack.'

'You've got 6.'

'6 days, Jack.'

There was silence at his end. Then he spoke again.

'All right. I'm leaving for the airport in an hour. Got business back east. I'll be back in 6 days.'

'Everything will be solved, baby.'

'Don't call me baby. What's this "baby" shit?'

'Just a manner of speaking . . .'

'You clean up this mess or I'll see you in hell, motherfucker!'

'You talking to me, Jack?'

I was holding a silent telephone. He'd hung up on me. The prick. Well . . . it was time to get busy . . .

34

So, there I was, parked outside of Bass's place, a third of a block down. It was evening, no it was night, about 8 p.m. Cindy's red Mercedes was in the drive. I had a hunch I was onto something. Something was going to happen. There was a smell in the air. I put my cigar out. I picked up my car phone and dialed out for the results of the 9th race. Lost again. Life was wearing. I felt oppressed, wasted. My feet hurt.

Cindy was probably in there watching something stupid on TV, crossing her warm legs and laughing at something inane and obvious. Then I began thinking about Jeannie Nitro and her five space buddies. They wanted to enlist me. I was no sell-out. I had to break up that gang. There had to be a way. Maybe if I could find the Red Sparrow, the Red Sparrow would sing me the answer. Was I crazy? Was all this happening?

I picked up the phone and dialed in John Barton. He was there.

'Listen, John, this is Belane. I'm having trouble closing in on the Red Sparrow. Maybe you better get another man.'

'No, Belane, I have faith in you, you'll do it.'

'You really think so?'

'I have no doubt of it.'

'Well, I'll stay on the case then.'

'Right.'

'I'll contact you if I get onto anything.'

'Do that. Good night.'

He hung up. Nice guy.

I started to relight my cigar. I almost spit it out. Cindy Bass was walking out of the house. She moved to her car. Got in.

Baby, baby, lead me to it.

She started up, turned on her lights, backed out of the drive. She swung around, headed north. I followed a half a block or so back. Then she turned onto the main boulevard, Pacific Coast Highway, to be exact. She headed south. I was about 3 car lengths back. She went across an intersection and the light turned red on me. I had to go through. It was close but no hit. I heard the horns and somebody called me an asshole. People lacked originality.

Then I was 3 car lengths behind her again. She was in the right hand lane. She began to slow down, then she turned into a driveway, a motel driveway. *Honeydunes Motel.* Sweet. She pulled in and parked at #9. I drove down to #7, parked, cut my lights and waited.

She climbed out, walked up the path, up to the door and knocked. The door opened and a guy stood there.

Ah, Cindy!

The guy stood in the light and I could make him out. He looked good. I don't mean to me. But to her, he must have. He was young. Blank smooth face with thin eyebrows, lots of hair. In fact, looked like he had a little pigtail. You know the kind. It was braided. A real jackass. They embraced in the doorway. Some kind of kiss. I heard Cindy laugh. Then she walked in and the door was closed.

I grabbed my camcorder and walked down to the office. Walked in. There was nobody there. There was a little desk. A bell. I hit the bell. Nothing. I hit the bell real hard, 6 times.

Somebody came walking out. An old fart. He was barefooted, dressed in a long nightgown and a stocking cap.

'Ah ha,' I said, 'you're ready for a good little old sleep, huh?'

'Maybe I am, maybe I'm not. What's it to you?'

'No offense, sir. I need a room. Do you have a vacancy?'

'You a pimp?'

'Oh, no, sir.'

'You sell drugs?'

'No, sir.'

'Wish you did. I need some coke.'

'I'm a bible salesman, sir.'

'That's disgusting!'

'Just trying to spread the word.'

'Well, don't spread that shit around me.'

'As you wish.'

'Fucking-A!'

'Well, sir, I need a room.'

'We got two. #8 and #3.'

'Did you say #8?'

'I said, #8 and #3. Don't you hear right?'

'I'll take #8.'

'35 bucks. Cash.'

I peeled the money off. He grabbed it, slammed down a key.

'Don't I get a receipt?'

'A what?'

'A receipt.'

'Spell it.'

'I can't.'

'Then you don't get it.'

I took the key, got out of there, walked down to #8, unlocked the door. Nice looking place. If you were homeless.

I found a glass in the kitchen. Brought it out and put it up against the wall facing #9. Luck. I could hear them.

'Billy,' I heard Cindy Bass say, 'let's not rush it. I want to talk a little first.'

'We can talk afterwards,' said Billy. 'I got this ramrod

here and I got to do something with it. I need flesh, not words!'

'I want to shower first, Billy.'

'Shower? What ya been doin', working in the garden?'

'Ah, Billy, you're so funny!'

'All right, go shower! I'll throw some icewater on this cobra!'

'Ah, Billy, hahaha!'

I smiled for the first time in weeks.

I was going to nail her.

35

I kept the drinking glass pressed to the wall and kept listening. I heard the shower water running. Poor Bass, he had been right. But everybody was right, and wrong, and upside-down. But what did it really matter who screwed who? It was finally all so drab. Fuck, fuck, fuck. Well, people got attached. Once you cut the umbilical cord they attached to other things. Sight, sound, sex, money, mirages, mothers, masturbation, murder and Monday morning hangovers.

I put the glass down, reached into my coat, found the half pint of gin, had a little nip. That always cleared the bugs out of the mind.

I began to think about another line of work. Here I

was going to bust in and camcord a screw scene and I
just didn't have any taste for it. It was just a job, the
rent, the booze, just waiting for the last day or night.
Marking time. What crap. I should have been a great
philosopher, I would have told them how foolish we
were, standing around sucking air in and out of our
lungs.

Damn, I was getting gloomy. I had another little hit
of gin, then put the glass back to the wall. She must
have just been coming out of the shower.

'Holy Christ,' he said, 'you're stacked like ten brick
shithouses!'

'Ah, Billy, you really think so?'

'I just told ya, didn't I?'

'You say the sweetest things, Billy.'

'I mean, looka the *size* of them breasts! You should
fall forward flat on your face but I guess it's your big
ass holds you back from doing that.'

'Oh, I don't have a big behind, Billy.'

'Baby, that's no behind! That there thing is a dump
truck full of jelly, jam and dumplings!'

'But, Billy, how about me? What about what's inside
of me?'

'Baby, can't you see this thing throbbing and leaping
around in front of me? *I'll* be *inside* of you!'

'Billy, I think I've changed my mind . . .'

'Baby, you got nothing to change! Come here! Climb
onto this Tower of Power!'

I pulled the glass from the wall, checked my camcorder, slipped out the door and moved over to the porch
of #9. Their door lock was easy. Got it open with my
Visa card.

I heard the springs begging for mercy in the bedroom. I switched the camcorder on and rushed in there. I got it. Billy was banging away like ten rabbits. Somehow, he noticed me. He rolled off and leaped to the floor. His mouth was hanging open. He was quite surprised and then he was quite pissed. Naturally.

He looked at me.

'Shit, what's this. What the FUCK is this?'

Cindy was sitting up in bed.

'He's a dick, Billy. He's crazy. He busted in on me and Jack working out and started camcording us. He's a real nut, Billy.'

I looked at her.

'You shut up, Cindy! This is it! I've finally nailed your ass!'

Billy moved toward me.

'Hey, buddy, you think I'm going to let you out of here alive?'

'Oh, hell yes, Billy boy, I'm not going to have any problem leaving, no problem at all.'

'Says who?'

'Says my friend here.'

I pulled the .32 out from my shoulder holster.

'That damned thing ain't going to stop me.'

'Try me, jerk!'

He kept slowly moving toward me.

'I've killed 3 men, Billy boy. 4 won't matter a twit!'

'Liar, liar,' he smiled, moving toward me, 'your mother's pants are on fire!'

'One more step, fart-head, and it's over!'

He took the step. I fired.

He just stood there. Then he reached down into his

belly button and pulled the bullet out. There wasn't any blood, not even a bruise.

'Bullets mean nothing to me,' he said, 'and neither do you.'

He took the gun out of my hand and tossed it into the corner of the bedroom.

'Now it's just me and you,' he said.

'Look, friend, let's talk this over. You can have the camcorder. I'm retiring from this business. You'll never see me again.'

'I know I won't because I'm going you kill you!'

'Yeah,' said Cindy from the bed, 'kill the filthy creep!'

I looked over.

'You stay out of this, Cindy, this is between the gentleman and myself.'

I looked at Billy.

'Right, Billy?'

'Right,' he answered.

Then he picked me up and hurled me across the room. I hit the wall and dropped to the floor.

'Billy,' I said, 'let's not let a big ass that half this town has been into cause hard feelings between us!'

Billy laughed and moved toward me.

36

Then it came to me. This guy was one of the space aliens. That's why he hadn't felt the bullet.

I got up and backed against the wall.

'I got your number, Billy!' I yelled.

He stopped. 'Yeah, tell me about it.'

'You're a space alien!'

Cindy laughed. 'I told you this guy was a nut!'

I looked at Cindy. 'This guy is nothing but a snake-like thing with fur and one big eye. He's hiding in what appears to be a human body, but it's a mirage.'

Billy just stood there looking at me.

'Where'd you meet this guy, Cindy?' I asked.

'At a bar. But I don't believe your shit. He's no space alien.'

'Ask him.'

Cindy laughed again. 'OK, Billy, are you a space alien?'

'Huh?' he answered.

'You see, you see!' I told Cindy.

Billy looked at her. 'You gonna believe this nut?'

'Of course not, Billy. Now, go ahead, finish him off!'

'OK, baby . . .'

Billy moved toward me. Then there was a flash of purple light in the room and Jeannie Nitro stood there.

'Jeannie,' said Billy, 'I . . .'

'Shut up, you bastard!' said Jeannie.

'What the hell's going on here?' Cindy asked, starting to get dressed. Billy was still balls-ass naked.

'You bastard,' said Jeannie, 'I told you that there would be no fraternizing with the humans!'

'Baby, I couldn't help myself, I got the hots. I was sitting in a bar one night and this number walked in.'

'Your orders were No Sex with the Earthlings!'

'Jeannie, you know that you're the one for me. It's just that you've been busy and all . . .'

'You've had it, Billy!' She pointed her right hand toward him.

'No, Jeannie, no!'

There was a purple flash and instantly Billy was turned into a furry snake with one moist eye and began wriggling rapidly across the floor. Once again Jeannie's right hand pointed at him, there was another flash and a roar and then Billy the space alien was gone.

'I can't believe what I've seen!' said Cindy.

'Yeah,' I said, 'I know.'

Then Jeannie looked at me. 'Don't forget, Belane, you've been selected for the Cause, the Cause of Zaros.'

'Yeah,' I said, 'I can't forget.'

Then there was a third flash of light and Jeannie was gone.

Cindy was now fully dressed but still in a state of shock.

'I can't believe what I've seen here.'

'Baby, Jack hired me to clean up your mess and that's what I've done.'

'I've got to get out of here!' she said.

'You do that. And don't forget what I've got on this camcorder here. You stay in line or I turn it over to Jack.'

'All right,' she sighed, 'you win.'

'I'm the greatest dick in LA. You gotta know that now.'

'Look, Belane, I've got something I can give you for that camcorder.'

'Huh?'

'You know what I mean.'

'No, no, Cindy, you can't buy me. Nice try, though.'

'Well, screw you, fat boy!' she said. She turned and walked toward the door. I watched those unbelievable haunches moving.

'Cindy!' I said, 'wait a minute!'

She turned, smiling. 'Yes?'

'Never mind. Go ahead . . .'

Then she was out the door.

I walked into the bathroom and relieved myself and I don't mean I had a bowel movement. But I was a true professional. Another case solved.

37

The next day at the office I got Jack Bass on the phone.

'You still want to divorce Cindy, Jack?'

'I dunno. You got anything on her?'

'Let's put it this way. The two gentlemen she had contact with are now dead.'

'Contact. What the hell do you mean by "contact"?'

'Jack, please, these guys are dead now, there was a Frenchman and a space alien.'

'A space alien? What kinda crap you feeding me?'

'No crap, Jack. We've been invaded by a few space aliens from Zaros. She met one of them in a bar. Pretty well-hung chap.'

'He's dead now?'

'Yeah, him and the Frenchman, like I said.'

'You kill people?'

'Jack, these guys are gone. Cindy's not going to play anymore. You can relax.'

'How do I know she's not going to play anymore?'

'Don't worry. I got an ace. She's not going to play.'

'You got something on your camcorder she doesn't want me to see, is that it?'

'Maybe. Maybe not. Let's just say I can nail her ass with this if she does.'

'But I want her to be with me because of me, not because of some blackmail.'

'Blackmail, schmackmail, Jack, she's not going to play anymore. I got rid of her contacts and she's gonna keep her panties on. What more can you ask? Maybe she'll even get to like you. Give her a chance to come around. She's young, she needed a fling, what the hell.'

'With a space alien?'

'Be glad. Nobody will ever know who he was. It's almost like it didn't happen.'

'But it did. You say he was well-hung? How well-hung was he?'

'Hard to tell. He was working . . .'

'You watched?'

'I stopped it.'

'How about the Frenchman? Was he well-hung too?'

'Jack, both those guys are dead. Forget it. You'll be getting my bill in the mail in a couple of days.'

'There's something about all this that doesn't rest well with me.'

'She's not going to play anymore, Jack.'

'But suppose she does?'

'She won't because she knows I can nail her ass.'

'There you go again. You weren't banging her, were you?'

'Jack, Jack, Jack, please! I'm a professional.'

'And these guys are dead? How do I know this?'

'Jack, you'll know by the way she behaves. Now stop worrying. You got anything else you want me to solve? I'm the best dick in LA.'

'I don't have anything right now.'

'OK, Jack, have a nice day.'

'Sure, sure . . .'

I hung up.

I opened the desk drawer and got out the vodka, had a hit. Things were working out. Now all I had to do was to find the Red Sparrow. And stop from getting too involved with the space aliens. Or Lady Death.

I had another hit of vodka. And allowed myself to feel all right. For a while.

38

Next I got John Barton on the phone. He ran a printing company up north.

'Belane here, John . . .'

'Good to hear from you, Nick. How's it going?'

'A little slow, John. I need some more information about this Red Sparrow.'

'Well, we want to make the Red Sparrow the logo of our company. Make it really well known. But now I've heard there is another Red Sparrow out there somewhere. We need to find it if it's there.'

'Is that all you're going on?'

'Well, maybe also a . . . hunch . . .'

'You ever seen this Red Sparrow?'

'I hear that it's been sighted.'

'You hear? You hear where?'

'Secret sources. I can't divulge too much.'

'Suppose I find this bird? What do you want me to do? Cage it?'

'No, just get me some real evidence that it exists. To satisfy my curiosity.'

'Suppose I never find this bird?'

'You'll find it if it's there. I have faith in you.'

'Listen, this is the screwiest case I've ever been on.'

'I've always told the world that you were a great detective. You'll prove it for me. You'll find the Red Sparrow.'

'All right, John. I'll work on it. But I'm not a kid anymore. I wake up tired. I think I've lost a few steps.'

'You're in your prime. You can do it.'

'All right, John, I'll give it a go ...'

'Great!'

I put the phone down. Well, that was it. But where would I begin?

I decided to try the nearest bar.

It was around 3 p.m. I found a stool and sat down. The bartender came up. Lonely looking guy. Didn't have any eyelids. Had little green crosses painted on his fingernails. Some kind of nut. There was no avoiding them. Most of the world was mad. And the part that wasn't mad was angry. And the part that wasn't mad or angry was just stupid. I had no chance. I had no choice. Just hang on and wait for the end. It was hard work. It was the hardest work imaginable. I forced myself to look at the bartender.

'Scotch and water,' I said.

He just stood there.

'Scotch and water,' I repeated.

'Oh,' he said. Then he trotted off.

I saw her walk in out of the corner of my eye. Why do they say 'corner of the eye'? Eyes have no corners. Anyhow, I saw her walk in. An old friend. She took the stool to my right.

'Hello, sucker,' she said, 'you buying?'

'Sure, baby.'

It was Lady Death.

'Hey, boy!' I yelled down at the barkeep, 'make that two!'

'Huh?' he asked.

'Make that two scotch and waters, please.'

'Uh, OK,' he said.

'Whatcha been doin', fat boy?' Lady asked.

'Solving cases, as per custom.'

'Meaning slow or never.'

'No, baby, no, you see, I'm the best dick in LA.'

'That's not saying much.'

'It beats churning butter left-handed.'

'Don't sass me, fat boy, or I'll take you out like a light bulb.'

'Sorry, baby, my nerves are shot. Maybe a drink will help.'

And there was the barkeep putting them down before us.

'What happened to your eyelids?' Lady asked him.

'My gas heater exploded this morning . . .'

'How ya gonna sleep tonight?'

'I'll wrap a towel around my head.'

'Couldn't you do that now?' I asked.

'Why?' he asked.

'Never mind . . .' I paid for the drinks.

I raised my drink. Lady lifted hers.

'Long life,' Lady said.

'Yeah, long life,' I said.

We clicked the glasses and drank.

I reordered . . .

* * *

We'd been sitting there about 30 minutes when some-body else walked in. Another woman. She walked around and sat herself on the stool to my left. Two women meant twice as much trouble as one woman. Now I had trouble on either side. I was in the vise. I was screwed.

The other woman was Jeannie Nitro.

I got the barkeep to make another scotch and water.

'Nicky,' she whispered, 'I've got to talk to you. Who's that bitch sitting with you?'

'You'd never guess,' I said.

Then Lady Death was whispering to me, 'Who's that bitch?'

'You'd never guess,' I said.

The drink came and Jeannie tossed it off.

'Well,' I said, 'I guess it's time for introductions . . .'

I turned to Lady Death.

'Lady, this is Jeannie Nitro . . .'

Then I turned to Jeannie.

'Jeannie, this is Lady . . . Lady . . .'

'Lady d'Heat,' Lady supplied.

They stared at each other.

Now this, I thought, could prove to be very interest-ing.

I waved the barkeep down for refills . . .

39

Here, basically, I was sitting between Space and Death. In the form of Woman. What chance did I have? Meanwhile, I was supposed to locate a Red Sparrow that maybe didn't exist. I felt very odd about everything. I had never expected to get tangled up like this. I hardly understood the why of it. What could I do?

Play it cool, fool, came the answer.

OK.

The drinks had arrived.

'Well, ladies, here's to you!'

We clicked glasses and had a hit.

Why couldn't I be just some guy sitting watching a baseball game? Involved in the outcome. Why couldn't I be a fry cook scrambling eggs and acting detached? Why couldn't I be a fly on some person's wrist, crawling along sublimely involved? Why couldn't I be a rooster in a chicken pen pecking at seed? Why this?

Jeannie nudged me with her elbow, whispered, 'Belane, I've got to talk to you . . .'

I put some bills on the bar. Then I looked at Lady Death.

'I hope this doesn't piss you but . . .'

'I know, fat boy, you've got to talk to the lady alone. Why should that piss me? I'm not in love with you.'

'But you always seem to be hanging around me, Lady.'

'I hang around everybody, Nick, you are just more aware of me.'

'Yeah. Yeah.'

'Well, you helped me with Celine . . .'

'Yes, Celine . . .'

'So, I'll leave you alone for a while with your lady. But only for a while. You and I have some unfinished business, so I'll be seeing you.'

'Lady d'Heat, I have no doubt of that . . .'

She finished her drink and rose from her stool. She turned and walked toward the door. Her beauty was foreboding. Then she was gone.

The barkeep came down for his money.

'Who was that?' he asked. 'I got kind of dizzy when she walked by.'

'Be glad you only felt dizzy,' I told him.

'What do you mean?' he asked.

'If I told you, you wouldn't believe it,' I said.

'Try me,' he said.

'I don't have to. Now look, give me a little space here, I want to talk to this lady.'

'All right. But just tell me one thing.'

'OK.'

'How come a fat ugly guy like you gets all the action?'

'It's because of the buttermilk I put on my waffles. Now, get the hell out of here.'

'Don't get fresh, buddy,' he said.

'You asked.'

'But you didn't have to get nasty!'

'If you think that was nasty, just keep hanging around.'

'Fuck you,' he said.

'That was brilliant,' I said. 'Now move off while you can.'

He slowly moved down to the end of the bar, stood there a moment, then scratched his ass.

I turned back to Jeannie.

'Sorry, baby, but I seem to get into these negative dialogues with almost every bartender I meet.'

'It's all right, Belane.'

She looked sad.

'Belane, I'm going to have to leave.'

'Oh, that's OK, but have one for the road.'

'No, I mean I'm going to have to leave, the people I have with me are going to have to leave . . . the earth. I don't know why, but I got kind of fond of you.'

'That's understandable,' I laughed, 'but why is your gang leaving the earth?'

'We've thought it over, it's just too awful. We don't want to colonize your earth.'

'What's too awful, Jeannie?'

'The earth. Smog, murder, the poisoned air, the poisoned water, the poisoned food, the hatred, the hopelessness, everything. The only beautiful thing about the earth is the animals and now they are being killed off, soon they will be gone except for pet rats and race horses. It's so sad, no wonder you drink so much.'

'Yeah, Jeannie. And don't forget our atomic stock-piles.'

'Yes, you've dug yourself in too deep, it seems.'

'Yes, we could be gone in two days or we might last another thousand years. We don't know which and so it's hard for most people to care about anything.'

'I'm going to miss you, Belane, *and* the animals . . .'

'I don't blame you for leaving, Jeannie . . .'

I saw the tears form in her eyes.

'Please don't cry, Jeannie, damn it all . . .'

She reached out for her drink, drank it down, looked at me with eyes I had never ever seen anywhere else nor would I ever see the like of them again.

'Goodbye, fat boy,' she smiled.

And then she was gone.

40

So, there I was the next day, back at my office. One assignment left: locate the Red Sparrow. Nobody was beating at my door with new work for me to do. That was fine. It was a time for a tabulation, a tabulation of myself. All in all, I had pretty much done what I had set out to do in life. I had made some good moves. I wasn't sleeping on the streets at night. Of course, there were a lot of good people sleeping in the streets. They weren't fools, they just didn't fit into the needed machinery of the moment. And those needs kept altering. It was a grim set-up and if you found yourself sleeping in your own bed at night, that alone was a precious victory over the forces. I'd been lucky but some of the moves I'd made had not been entirely without thought. But all in all it was a fairly horrible world and I felt sad, often, for most of the people in it.

Well, to hell with it. I pulled out the vodka and had a hit.

Often the best parts of life were when you weren't doing anything at all, just mulling it over, chewing on it. I mean, say that you figure that everything is senseless, then it can't be quite senseless because you are aware that it's senseless and your awareness of sense-lessness almost gives it sense. You know what I mean? An optimistic pessimism.

The Red Sparrow. It was like the search for the Holy Grail. Maybe the water was too deep for me. And too hot.

I had another hit of vodka.

There was a rap on the door. I took my feet off the desk.

'Come on in.'

The door opened and there stood this guy, slight of build, dressed in raggedy-ass clothing. There was a smell to him. Something like kerosene. I wasn't sure. He had small slitted eyes. He moved toward me sidewise. Then he stopped, right at the edge of my desk, leaned forward. He had a slight head twitch.

'Belane,' he said.

'Perhaps,' I answered.

'I got it all here for you,' he said.

'Good,' I said, 'now take it the hell out of here.'

'Easy, Belane, I got the word.'

'Yeah? What's the word?'

'Red Sparrow.'

'Tell me more.'

'We know you're looking for it.'

' "We," huh? Who's "we"?'

'Can't say.'

I got up, walked around the desk, grabbed him by his pitiful shirt front.

'Suppose I make you say? Suppose I kick it out of you?'

'Can't. I don't know.'

Somehow, I believed him. I let go. He almost fell to the floor. I walked around, sat behind my desk again.

'My name's Amos,' he said, 'Amos Redsdale. I can put you on the road to the Sparrow. You want it?'

'What is it?'

'An address. She knows about the Sparrow.'

'How much?'

'75 dollars.'

'Screw you, Amos.'

'OK, you don't want it? I gotta go. I gotta make the first post. I got a tip on the daily double.'

'50 bucks.'

'60,' said Amos.

'All right, let me have the address.'

I dug out 3 twenties and he handed me a slip of paper. I opened it and read it. It said: 'Deja Fountain, apt. 9, 3234 Rudson Drive. W.L.A.'

'Look, Amos, you could write any kind of shit here you want. How do I know this is any good?'

'You just go there, Belane. It's good stuff.'

'For the sake of your ass, Amos, it had better be.'

'I gotta make first post,' he said. Then he turned, walked to the door and was gone.

And I was sitting there out 60 bucks and holding a piece of paper.

41

I waited until that night, drove over, parked outside. Nice neighborhood. Definition of a nice neighborhood: a place you couldn't afford to live in. I had a nip of vodka, slid out of the seat, locked the door and walked up to the apartment complex. I pushed the button by the nameplate: Deja Fountain. The voice came through, sweet but with just an edge: 'Yes?'

'For Deja Fountain. Regarding the Red Sparrow. Sent by Amos Redsdale. My name is Nick Belane.'

'Sir, I don't know what the hell you are talking about.'

'Shit.'

'What?'

'Nothing. I've been taken . . .'

'I was just jesting with you, Nicky. Please enter.'

There was a loud buzzing sound. I tried the front door. It opened. I walked along the plush rug until I found apartment 9. What was it about 9? There seemed something dangerous about it. But most numbers worried me. I only liked 3, 7 and 8 or combinations thereof.

I pressed the button. I heard footsteps. Then the door opened.

She was a stunner. In a red dress. Green eyes. Long dark brown hair. Young. Class. Ass. A smell of mint. Her lips smiled.

'Mr. Belane, please come in.'

I followed her into the room. Then there was a hard object in my back.

'Freeze, motherfucker! Except your arms! Stretch them up! See if you can reach the ceiling, mother-fucker!'

'You black?' I asked.

'What?'

'Only blacks say "motherfucker." '

He was patting me down. He found my piece, took it.

'All right, you can turn around now, Mr. Belane.'

I turned and looked at him. Big guy but white.

'But you're white,' I said.

'So are you,' he said.

'Well, I'll be a motherfucker,' I said.

'That's up to you. You can have your piece when you leave.'

I followed Deja into another room. She waved me to a chair.

It was a big room. Cold. Felt dangerous.

Deja placed herself on the couch, pulled out a small cigar, unsheathed it, licked it up a touch, bit off the end, lit up, exhaling a sexy blue plume of smoke. She fixed me with her green eyes.

'I understand you're looking for the Red Sparrow.'

'Yes, for a client.'

'Who is?'

'That's confidential.'

'I have the feeling that we can be good friends, Mr. Belane, very good friends.'

'You do, huh?'

'You're a handsome man, in your way, you must know that. You have that well-lived-in look. It's quite becoming. Most men don't live well at all, they just wear down.'

'Is that right?'

'You can call me Deja.'

'Deja.'

'Ummm . . . why don't you come over here and sit near me?'

I moved it over and dropped it near her on the couch. She smiled.

'Care for a drink?'

'Sure. Got a scotch and soda?'

'Bernie,' she said, 'one scotch and soda, please.'

A few moments passed and here came the mother-fucker who had taken my piece. He set the drink down before me on the coffee table.

'Thank you, Bernie.'

He moved off, vanished.

I had a hit of the scotch. Not bad. Not bad.

'Mr. Belane,' she said, 'I've been told to tell you that you must forget all about the Red Sparrow.'

'I never drop a case unless my client so desires.'

'You'll drop this one, Mr. Belane.'

'Uh-uh.'

'Does my smoking this cigar offend you?'

'Uh-uh.'

'Would you like to try a drag?'

'Uh huh.'

Deja handed me the cigar. I took a good pull, inhaled, exhaled, gave the cigar back. The room was clear for a moment, then the walls began to shift a bit, the rug rose up, fell back down. A shot of blue light flashed in front of me. Then her mouth was on mine. She kissed me, then pulled away. She laughed.

'How long has it been since you've had a woman, Belane?'

'I can't remember . . .'

She laughed again and then her mouth was on mine again. It had been a long time. Her tongue slithered into my mouth like a snake. Her body was like a snake.

Then I heard footsteps, a voice: 'HOLD IT!'

It was Bernie. He was standing there with two guns, one in each hand. One of the guns I recognized as mine.

'OK, Bernie, OK,' I said.

Bernie was inhaling heavily as if there were no oxygen in the air. He was staring at Deja. His eyes were misted.

'DEJA,' he said, 'YOU KNOW THAT I LOVE YOU! I'LL KILL HIM! I'LL KILL YOU! I'LL KILL MYSELF!'

I was in a perfect position. I swung my right leg up and got him right between the nodules. He screamed and dropped, holding his center. I picked up the guns, put one in my holster, held the other in my right hand. I lifted him with my left and dropped him into a chair. I pulled his head back by the hair until his mouth fell open. Then I slid the gun into his mouth.

'Suck on this awhile, chap, while I think about what I'm going to do.'

Bernie made a gurgling sound.

'Don't kill him!' said Deja. 'Please don't kill him!'

'What do you know about the Red Sparrow, motherfucker?' I asked him.

He didn't answer.

I shoved the gun deeper into his mouth. Then I heard
him fart. It was a loud fart. And a stinking one. I pulled
the gun out and threw him to the floor.

'That was disgusting! *Don't ever do that again!'*

I turned and looked at Deja.

'Does he have a room here?'

'Yes.'

I looked at Bernie.

'Now, you go to your room and stay there until I tell
you to come out!'

Bernie nodded.

'Now get going,' I told him.

He got to his feet and slumped off, went around the
corner. Soon I heard a door close.

Deja had put out her cigar. She was no longer
smiling.

'OK, baby,' I said, 'let's get back to where we left
off.'

'I don't want to.'

'What? Why? You had your tongue halfway down
my esophagus.'

'I'm afraid of you, you're too violent.'

'But he said he was going to kill you, didn't you hear
him?'

'He probably didn't mean it.'

'You don't go on "probably" when love and guns are
in hand.'

Deja sighed.

'I'm worried about Bernie. He's sitting in his room all alone.'

'Doesn't he have a TV? Crossword puzzles? A comic book?'

'Please, Mr. Belane, please leave!'

'Baby, I want to get to the bottom of this Red Sparrow thing.'

'Not tonight . . . not tonight.'

'When then?'

'Tomorrow night. Same time.'

'Send Bernie to a movie or something.'

'All right.'

I reached down, grabbed my drink, finished it off. I left her sitting on the couch, staring at the rug. I closed the door behind me, walked down the hall, out the front door and back to my car. I got in and kicked the engine over. I sat and let it warm up. It was a warm moonlight night. And I still had a hard-on.

42

I drove down to a bar where I hadn't been in trouble yet – Blinky's. It looked fair at first glance: lots of leather booths, fools, darkness, smoke. A congenial deadliness floated in the air. I found a booth, sat down. Waitress arrived dressed in some silly outfit – pink playsuit with cotton pushing up her breasts. She smiled

a horrible smile, showed one gold tooth. Her eyes read
empty.

'What'll it be, honey?' her voice grated.

'Two bottles of beer. No glass.'

'Two bottles, honey?'

'Yeah.'

'What brand?'

'Something Chinese.'

'Chinese?'

'Two bottles of Chinese beer. No glass.'

'Can I ask you something?'

'Yes.'

'You gonna drink both those beers?'

'I hope so.'

'Then why don't you drink one, then order another?
Stay cold that way.'

'I just want to do it this way. There's a reason, I
guess.'

'You find out that reason, honey, you tell me . . .'

'Why should I tell you? Maybe I want to keep it to
myself.'

'Sir, you know, we don't have to serve you. We
reserve the right to refuse service to anybody.'

'You mean, you won't serve me because I'm ordering
two Chinese beers and not telling you why?'

'I didn't say we wouldn't serve you. I said we reserve
the right not to.'

'Look, the reason is security, a subconscious need for
security. I had a rotten childhood. Two bottles at once
fills a void that needs filling. Maybe. I'm not sure.'

'Honey, I'm going to tell you something. You need a
shrink.'

'All right. But until I get one, can I have two bottles of Chinese beer?'

A big guy in a dirty white apron walked up.

'What's the trouble here, Betty?'

'This guy wants two bottles of Chinese beer. Without a glass.'

'Betty, he's probably waiting for a friend.'

'He doesn't have a friend, Blinky.'

Blinky looked at me. He was another big fat guy. He was two big fat guys.

'Don't you have a friend?' he asked me.

'No,' I answered.

'Then what do you want with two bottles of Chinese beer?'

'I want to drink them.'

'Why don't you order one, finish it, then order another?'

'I'd rather do it this way.'

'I never heard of that,' said Blinky.

'Why can't I do it? Is it against the law?'

'No, it's just strange, that's all.'

'I told him he needs a shrink,' said Betty.

They both stood there looking at me. I took out a cigar and lit it up.

'That thing stinks,' said Blinky.

'So do your excreta,' I said.

'What?'

'Bring me,' I said, 'three bottles of Chinese beer. No glass.'

'This guy is a nut,' said Blinky.

I looked at him and laughed.

Then I said, 'Don't talk to me again. And don't do

anything, anything at all to irritate me or I'll blow your lips right off your fucking face, buddy boy.'

Blinky froze. He looked like he was going to have a bowel movement.

Betty stood there.

A minute passed. Then Betty said, 'What'll I do, Blinky?'

'Get him three bottles of Chinese beer. No glass.'

Betty left for the beers.

'Now you,' I said to Blinky, 'you sit yourself down across from me. I want you to watch me drinking these three Chinese beers.'

'Sure,' he said, sliding himself, somehow, into the booth across from me.

He was sweating. All three of his chins were trembling.

'Blinky,' I asked him, 'you haven't seen the Red Sparrow, have you?'

'The Red Sparrow?'

'Yes, the Red Sparrow.'

'Haven't seen it,' said Blinky.

Betty was arriving with the Chinese beers.

At last.

43

So there I was the next night, standing outside of the apartment complex. My shoes were shined and I'd only had 3 or 4 beers. A light, slightly ominous rain was falling. 'God is pissing,' we used to say when it rained when I was a kid. I felt tired, I mean in body and mind. I wanted out of the game. I wanted to retire. Say to some place like Vegas. Hanging around the gaming tables, looking wise. Watching fools blow fortunes. That was my idea of a good time. Relaxing under the lights as the grave yawned open for me. But, hell, I didn't have any money. And I had to find the Red Sparrow. I pressed the buzzer to apartment 9. I waited. I pressed the buzzer again. Nothing. Oh my. Oh my my my. I didn't want to think about it. Had they skipped? Deja and that motherfucker. I should have closed on them last night. Had I let them slip?

I lit my cigar with one hand, worked the door jimmy with the other. It slid open and I entered the hall. I walked down to 9. Pressed my ear to the door. Nothing. Not even the rustle of a mouse. Oh my. God damn it. I worked the door open and entered. Walked straight to the bedroom, opened the closet. Empty. Clothes gone. Nothing but lonely hangers. What an awful sight. My first link to the Red Sparrow now turned into 32 empty hangers. I had lost it. As a dick I was a fool. I thought faintly about suicide, dismissed that, reached into my coat, found the pint, had a hit of vodka, spit out my cigar.

Then I turned around, walked out of there, down the hall and along the hall until I found what I wanted. The door marked:

MANAGER, M. TOHIL

I knocked.

'Yeah?' came this reply. Sounded like another big guy.

'Flowers, Mr. Tohil. Flower delivery for M. Tohil!'

'How'd you get in here?'

'The front door was open, Mr. Tohil.'

'Impossible!'

'Mr. Tohil, a lady was leaving and I walked in the door as she walked out.'

'You're not supposed to do that.'

'I didn't know that. What was I supposed to do?'

'You're supposed to buzz me from outside and tell me who you are and what you want.'

'All right, Mr. Tohil. I'll go outside and buzz you and tell you that I have a flower delivery for you. Will that be all right?'

'Never mind, boy. Here . . .'

The door swung open. I jumped inside, kicked the door closed and grabbed him by the belt. I had a handful. He was a *big* guy. Needed a shave. Smelled a little like sulfur. Tipped the scales about 240.

'What the fuck you doing? Where are the flowers? Take your hand off my god-damned belt!'

'Easy, Tohil,' I let go of him, 'I'm a private investigator, fully licensed. I want to know the whereabouts of Deja Fountain, apartment 9.'

'Kiss my ass, buddy, and get the hell out of here.'

I backed off.

'Easy, Mr. Tohil. I just want this information, then I'll go.'

'The information is private and you'll go without it. I'm moving you out of here now!'

'I've got a black belt, Tohil. That's a lethal weapon. Don't force me to use it!'

He laughed and moved a step toward me.

'Hold it right there!' I yelled.

He stopped.

'Tohil, I've got to locate the Red Sparrow, and Deja Fountain ties in with the solution. I've got to know where she and her boy have gone.'

'They didn't leave a forwarding address,' he said. 'Now get out of here before I fart in your face!'

I slipped the .32 out and leveled it at his belly.

'WHERE'S DEJA FOUNTAIN?' I yelled.

'Screw you,' he said, moving toward me.

'Stop right there!' I commanded.

He kept coming, he was a fool. I panicked, pulled the trigger.

The gun jammed.

Then he had his hands about my throat. They were the size of hams, hams with huge, dumb, strong, relentless fingers. I couldn't breathe. Large flashes of light roared in my head behind my eyes. I pounded my knee into his groin. Nothing happened. He was a freak. His sexual organs were some place else, maybe up under one of his arm pits. I was helpless. I could feel death in the air. But my past life didn't flash before me. Just a voice in my head said, 'You need a new tire on the right rear . . .' Stupid, stupid. And I was finished, done. It was over for me.

Then, suddenly I felt the hands let go. I staggered back, sucking in air from the stratosphere and everywhere else.

I looked at Tohil. He didn't look good. He didn't look good at all. He was looking at me but he wasn't looking at me. I saw him grab his left arm. He held his left arm and this awfully pained look crossed his face. He gasped, looked up and fell to the floor.

I went over, bent over him, felt his pulse. Nothing. He was gone. Bye bye.

I walked over, sat in a chair. And there on the couch across from me, there she was: Lady Death. Never had she looked so good. What a babe. Never let you down. Better than gold. She smiled.

'How ya doin', Belane?'

'Can't complain, exactly, Lady.'

She was dressed completely in black. She looked good in black. Also red.

'Better watch your weight, Belane. You've been eating too many french fries, mashed potatoes, desserts . . . you've been sucking at beer bottles . . .'

'Yeah. Well . . . yeah . . .'

She smiled again. Perfect strong teeth. She could bite through a plumber's monkey wrench.

'Well,' she said, 'I've got to go. Some more business near at hand.'

'Anybody I know?'

'You know a Harry Dobbs?'

'I don't think so.'

'Well, if you do, forget him.'

Then she was gone. Like that.

I walked over to Tohil, dug for his wallet. There was a 50, 2 twenties, a 5 and a one. I slipped them into my right pants pocket. I walked to the door, opened it, closed it and walked down the hall. Nobody around. I got to the front door, stepped outside. The light rain was still falling. It felt good against my face. I inhaled, sighed, moved toward my car. It was still there. I walked around to the rear of it and checked the right rear tire. Sure enough, it was bald. I needed new rubber.

44

So, there I was depressed again. I drove back to my place, got in and opened a bottle of scotch. I was back with my old friend, scotch and water. Scotch is a drink you don't take to right off. But after you work with it a while it kind of works its magic on you. I find a special touch of warmth to it that whiskey doesn't have. Anyhow, I had the glooms and I sat in a chair with the 5th at my side. I didn't turn on the TV, I found that when you felt bad that son-of-a-bitch only made you feel worse. Just one vapid face after another, it was endless. An endless procession of idiots, some of them famous. The comedians weren't funny and the drama was 4th grade. There wasn't much to turn to for me, except the scotch.

The light rain had become a hard rain and I sat there listening to it belt against the roof.

I should never have let those fuckers slip away. And I knew I'd never find my original informant again. I was back at the beginning. The Red Sparrow had vanished from my stupid grasp. Here I was 55 years old and still fumbling in the dark. How long could I stay in the game? Did the inept deserve anything but a kick in the ass? My old man had told me, 'Get into anything where they hand you the money first and then hope to get it back. That's banking and insurance. Take the real thing and give them a piece of paper for it. Use their money, it will keep coming. *Two* things drive them: greed and fear. *One* thing drives you: opportunity.' Seemed like good advice. Only my father died broke.

I poured a new scotch.

Hell, I'd even failed with women. Three wives. Nothing really wrong each time. It all got destroyed by petty bickering. Railing about nothing. Getting pissed-off over anything and everything. Day by day, year by year, grinding. Instead of helping each other you just sliced away, picked at this or that. Goading. Endless goading. It became a cheap contest. And once you got into it, it became habitual. You couldn't seem to get out. You almost didn't want to get out. And then you did get out. All the way.

So, now, here I was. Sitting listening to the rain. If I died right now there wouldn't be one tear dropped anywhere in the world. Not that I wanted that. But it was odd. How alone could a sucker get? But there was a world full of old farts like me. Sitting listening to the rain, wondering where it all went. That's when you knew you were old, when you sat wondering where it went.

Well, it doesn't go anywhere, it's not supposed to. I was three quarters dead. I flicked on the TV. There was a commercial. LONELY? DEPRESSED? CHEER UP. PHONE ONE OF OUR BEAUTIFUL LADIES. THEY DESIRE TO SPEAK TO YOU. CHARGE IT TO YOUR MASTER OR VISA CARD. SPEAK TO KITTY OR FRANCI OR BLANCA. PHONE 800-435-8745.

They showed the girls. Kitty looked best. I took a hit of scotch and dialed the number.

'Yeah?' It was a man's voice. Sounded mean.

'Kitty, please.'

'You 21 or over?'

'Over,' I said.

'Master or Visa?'

'Visa.'

'Gimme your number and expiration date. Also, address, phone number, social security and your driver's license number.'

'Hey, how do I know you won't use this information for your own good? I mean, like screwing me around? Using this info for your own gain?'

'Hey, buddy, you want to talk to Kitty?'

'I guess so . . .'

'We advertise on TV. We been in business for 2 years.'

'All right, let me dig this stuff out of my wallet.'

'Buddy, if you don't want us, we don't want you.'

'What's Kitty going to talk to me about?'

'You'll like it.'

'How do you know I'll like it?'

'Hey, buddy . . .'

'All right, all right, wait a minute . . .'

I gave him the info. There was quite a pause while they cleared my credit. Then I heard a voice.

'Hi, baby, this is Kitty!'

'Hello, Kitty, my name is Nick.'

'Oooh, your voice is so *sexy*! I'm getting a little excited!'

'Nah, my voice isn't sexy.'

'Oh, you're just being modest!'

'No, Kitty, I'm not modest . . .'

'You know, I feel very *close* to you! I feel like I'm curled up in your lap, I'm looking up at you with my eyes. I have large blue eyes. You're leaning close, like you're about to kiss me!'

'That's crap, Kitty, I'm sitting here alone sucking on a scotch and listening to the rain.'

'Listen, Nick, you have to use your imagination just a little. Let go and you'll be surprised what we can do together. Don't you like my voice? Don't you find it a little . . . ah, sexy.'

'Yeah, a little but not too much. You sound like you got a cold. You got a cold?'

'Nick, Nick, my dear boy, I'm too *hot* to have a cold!'

'What?'

'I said, I'm too *hot* to have a cold!'

'Well, you sound like you've got a cold. Maybe you smoke too many cigarettes.'

'I only smoke *one thing*, Nick!'

'What's that, Kitty?'

'Can't you guess?'

'Nah . . .'

'Look down at yourself, Nick.'

'OK.'

'What do you see?'

'Drink. Telephone . . .'

'What else, Nicky?'

'My shoes . . .'

'Nick, what's that *big thing* sticking out there as you talk to me?'

'Oh, that! That's my *gut*!'

'Keep talking to me, Nick. Keep listening to my voice, think of me there in your lap, my dress slipped up a bit, my knees and thighs showing. I have long blond hair. It showers down over me. Think of all that, Nick, think of it. . .'

'All right . . .'

'OK, now what do you *see*?'

'Same things: telephone, my shoes, my drink, my gut . . .'

'Nick, you're bad! I've got a good mind to come over there and spank you! Or maybe I'll let you *spank me*!'

'What?'

'*Spanky, spanky, Nick*!'

'Kitty . . .'

'Yes?'

'Will you pardon me for a minute? I have to go to the bathroom.'

'Oh Nick, I know what you're going to *do*! But you don't have to go to the *bathroom* to do it, you can do it right over the *phone* while you're *talking* to me!'

'No, I can't, Kitty. I gotta take a piss.'

'Nick,' she said, 'you can consider our conversation over!'

She hung up.

I went to the bathroom and urinated. As I did, I could still hear the rain going. Well, it had been a lousy conversation but at least it had taken my mind off of the Red Sparrow and other matters. I flushed, washed my hands, stared into the mirror, winked at myself and walked back out to the scotch.

45

So there I was, back at the office the next day. I was feeling unfulfilled and, frankly, rather crappy about everything. I wasn't going anywhere and neither was the rest of the world. We were all just hanging around waiting to die and meanwhile doing little things to fill the space. Some of us weren't even doing little things. We were vegetables. I was one of those. I don't know what kind of vegetable I was. I felt like a turnip. I lit a cigar, inhaled, and pretended that I knew what the hell.

The phone rang. I picked it up.

'Yeah?'

'Mr. Belane, you have been selected as one of our prize winners. Your prize can be a TV set, a trip to Somalia, $5,000 or a folding umbrella. We have a free room for you, a free breakfast. All you have to do is attend one of our seminars where we will offer you an unlimited real estate value . . .'

'Hey, buddy,' I said.

'Yes, sir?'

'Go hump a rabbit!'

I hung up. I stared at the phone. Deathly damned thing. But you needed it to call 911. You never knew.

I needed a vacation. I needed 5 women. I needed to get the wax out of my ears. My car needed an oil change. I'd failed to file my damned income tax. One of the stems had broken off of my reading glasses. There were ants in my apartment. I needed to get my teeth cleaned. My shoes were run down at the heels. I had insomnia. My auto insurance had expired. I cut myself every time I shaved. I hadn't laughed in 6 years. I tended to worry when there was nothing to worry about. And when there was something to worry about, I got drunk.

The phone rang again. I picked it up.

'Belane?' this voice asked.

'Maybe,' I answered.

'Maybe my ass,' the voice went on, 'either you're Belane or you're not Belane.'

'All right, you got me. I'm Belane.'

'All right, Belane, we hear you're looking for the Red Sparrow.'

'Yeah? What's your source?'

'Our source is private.'

'So are your parts but you can expose them.'

'We choose not to.'

'All right,' I said, 'so what's the play?'

'$10,000 and we'll put the Red Sparrow into your hand.'

'I don't have the ten.'

'We can put you in touch with someone who can let you have it.'

'Really?'

'Really, Belane. Only 15% interest. A month.'

'But I don't have any collateral.'

'Sure you have.'

'What?'

'Your life.'

'That all? Let's talk.'

'Sure, Belane. We'll be at your office. Ten minutes.'

'How'll I know it's you?'

'We'll tell you.'

I hung up.

Ten minutes later there was a knock on the door. A loud knock. The whole door rattled and shook. I checked my desk drawer for the luger. It was there, pretty as a picture. A nude one.

'It's open, for Christ's sake, come on in!'

The door swung open. A huge body blocked the light. An ape with a cigar and a light pink suit. He was with two smaller apes.

I motioned him to a chair. He sat in it, completely filling it. The chair legs gave a bit. One ape flanked him on each side.

The main ape belched, leaned forward a bit toward me.

'I'm Sanderson,' he said, 'Harry Sanderson. These,' he nodded toward his cohorts, 'are my boys.'

'Your sons?' I asked.

'Boys, boys,' he said.

'Yeah,' I said.

'You need us,' said Sanderson.

'Yeah,' I said.

'The Red Sparrow,' said Sanderson.

'Are you connected with that babe and her mongrel boy who skipped their apartment the other night?'

'I ain't tied to no babe,' he said. 'I just use them for one thing.'

'What's that?' I asked.

'To mop my poop deck.'

Each of his apes giggled. They had thought that cute.

'I don't think that's cute,' I said.

'We don't care,' said Sanderson, 'what you think.'

'That makes sense,' I said. 'Now, let's talk about the Red Sparrow.'

'$10,000,' said Sanderson.

'Like I said, I don't have it.'

'And like I said, we get a Loaner to give it to you, easy terms, 15% a month.'

'OK, get me the Loaner.'

'We're the Loaner.'

'You?'

'Yeah, Belane. We give it to you, you then hand it back. Then you pay 15% of ten grand each month until the loan is fully repaid. All you do is sign this piece of paper. No money really changes hands. We just keep it, to save you from handing it back.'

'And for this, you'll . . .'

'Put the Red Sparrow right in your hand.'

'How do I know this?'

'Know what?'

'That you'll put the Sparrow in my hand.'

'You gotta trust us.'

'That's what I thought you said.'

'You don't, Belane?'

'What?'

'Don't trust us.'

'Sure but it's better you trust me.'

'Like what?'

'Put the Sparrow in my hand *first*.'

'What? What do we look like to you, a bunch of wooden dummies?'

'Well, yes . . .'

'Don't get wise, Belane. You've got to trust us if you want to see the Red Sparrow. It's your only chance. Think about it. You've got 24 hours.'

'All right, let me think.'

'Think, Belane,' the big ape in the pink suit stood up. 'Think real good. And let us know. You've got 24 hours. After that, the deal is off. Forever.'

'OK,' I said.

He turned around and one of his apes ran ahead and opened the door for him. The other one stood there looking at me. Then they all left. And I sat there. I had no idea. The ballgame was in my lap. And the clock was running. What the hell. I reached into my desk for the pint of vodka. It was lunch time.

46

Well, what are you going to do? I worried so much that I fell asleep at my desk. When I awakened it was dark. I got up, put on my coat and my derby and got out of there. I got in my car and drove 5 miles west. Just to do it. Then I parked it and looked around. I was parked in front of a bar. *Hades*, said the neon sign. I got out of the car, went in. There were 5 people in there. 5 miles, 5 people. Everything was coming up 5s. There was a bartender, a babe and these 3 thin limp stupid kids. The kids seemed to have shoeblack in their hair. They smoked long cigarettes and sneered at me, at everything. The babe was at one end of the bar, the kids at the other, the bartender in the middle. I finally got the bartender's attention by picking up an ashtray and dropping it twice. He blinked and moved toward me. His head looked like a frog's head. But he didn't hop, he stumbled toward me, stopped in front of me.

'Scotch and water,' I told him.

'You want the water in the scotch?'

'I said, "Scotch *and* water." '

'Huh?'

'Scotch and water, separately, please.'

The 3 kids were looking at me. The one in the middle spoke.

'Hey, old man, you want some pain?'

I just looked at him and smiled.

'We give free pain,' the one in the middle said. They all sneered, they all kept sneering.

The bartender arrived with my scotch and water.

'I think I'll come down and drink your drink,' the same one spoke again.

'You touch my drink and I'll break you in half like a piece of dry shit.'

'Oh my my my,' he said.

'Oh my,' said the second.

'Oh my,' said the third.

I drained the scotch and skipped the water.

'Old man thinks he's tough,' said the one in the middle.

'Maybe we ought to see how tough he is,' said another.

'Yes,' said the last.

God, how boring they were. Like almost everybody else. Nothing new, nothing fresh any more. Dead, flat. Like the movies.

'Give me the same thing.' I told the bartender.

'Was that a scotch and water?'

'It was.'

'That old man don't look like much to me,' said the one in the middle.

'Doesn't,' I said.

'Doesn't what?'

'Old man *doesn't* look like much.'

'Then you agree with us?'

'Correcting you. And I hope it's the last correction I have to make tonight.'

The bartender arrived with my drink. Then, he left.

'Maybe we can correct your ass,' said the one who had been doing most of the talking.

I ignored that one.

'Maybe we'll stick your head up your ass,' said one of the others.

Boring damned people. All over the earth. Propagating more boring damned people. What a horror show. The earth swarmed with them.

'Maybe we'll make you suck a carrot,' said one of them.

'Maybe he'd like to suck three carrots,' said one of the others.

I didn't say anything. I drained my scotch, had a water, stood up, nodded to the back of the bar.

'Oh, look he wants to see us outside!'

'Maybe he wants our carrots!'

'Let's go see!'

I walked out toward the back. I heard them behind me. Then I heard the click of a switch blade opening. I turned in time to kick it out of his hand. Then I gave him a chop behind the ear. He dropped and I stepped over him. The other two turned and started running. They ran down through the bar and out the front entrance. I let them go. I walked back to the other kid. He was still out. I picked him up, carried him over my shoulder, took him outside. I stretched him out on a bus bench on his back. Then I took off his shoes and threw them down a storm drain. Ditto his wallet. Then I went back inside, went back and got the switch blade, pocketed it, went back to my stool, ordered another drink.

I heard the babe cough. She was lighting a cigarette.

'Mister,' she said, 'I liked that, I like real men.'

I ignored that.

'I'm Trachea,' she said.

She picked up her drink and came and sat down next to me. She had on too much perfume and a week's worth of lipstick.

'We could get to know each other,' she said.

'It wouldn't pay off, it would only be stupid.'

'What makes you say that?'

'Experience.'

'Maybe you met all the wrong kinds of women?'

'Maybe I'm attached to that.'

'I could be the right one.'
'Sure.'
'Buy me a drink.'
Mine was arriving.
'A drink for Trachea,' I told the barkeep.
'Gin and tonic, Bobby . . .'
Bobby toddled off.
'You haven't told me your name?' she lisped.
'David.'
'Oh, I like that. I once knew a David.'
'What happened to him?'
'I forget.'
Trachea leaned her flank against me. She was about
25 pounds overweight.
'You're cute,' she said.
'Why?' I asked.
'Ah, I dunno . . .' She paused. 'You like me?'
'Well, not really.'
'You should. I'm good.'
'What at? You take shorthand?'
'No, but I make short things long.'
'Like what?'
'You know!'
'No, I don't.'
'Guess.'
'Balloons?'
'You're funny.'
'I've been told.'
Her drink arrived. She took a sip.
The more I looked at her the less enamored I became.
'Damn it,' she said, 'my lighter!'
She opened her purse and began pulling things out. A

beer bottle opener. Three shades of lipstick. Chewing gum. A whistle. And . . . what?

'I found it!' she said, holding up the lighter. She tapped out a cigarette, lit it.

'What's that thing there?'

'Where?'

'There. On the bar. That red thing.'

I pointed.

'Oh,' she said, 'that's my sparrow.'

'Is it alive? Was it alive? Ever?'

'No, silly, it's stuffed. I got it at a pet shop today. It's for my kitty. It's my catnip sparrow. Kitty loves them.'

'Oh, hell, put it away.'

'David, you got excited there for a minute! Do birds turn you on?'

'Just the Red Sparrow.'

'You want it?'

'No, it's all right.'

'I got some more catnip sparrows at my place. You can meet my kitty.'

'No, it's all right, Trachea. I've got to get going.'

'All right, David, but you don't know what you're missing.'

I got up, walked down the bar, tossed some bills to the bartender and walked out. The punk was no longer on the bench. I got into my car, pulled out and headed into traffic. It was about ten p.m. The moon was up and my life was slowly going nowhere.

47

The next day I was sitting in the office. The door kicked open and there was Harry Sanderson and his two monkeys. This time Sanderson was dressed in a light purple suit. His taste in colors was freaky. I knew a babe like that once, she had a way of wearing those weird colors. Like we'd go out to a restaurant to eat and everybody would turn and look at her. Problem was, she wasn't much to look at. Even with a hangover and a 3-day beard I looked better than she did. Anyhow, back to Sanderson –

'Punk,' he said, 'your 24 hours are up. You still diddling with your weenie or you made your mind up?'

'I'm still diddling with my weenie.'

'You want the Red Sparrow or not?'

'I want it. But you guys remind me of these guys who worked over my aunt in Illinois.'

'Your aunt? What the fuck's this about your aunt?'

'She had a leaky roof.'

'That right?'

'Yeah. These guys came by and told her they'd fix her roof, they had a new super sealant. They had her sign a piece of paper, write out a check and then they climbed up there.'

'Up where, punk?'

'The roof. They got up there and poured used motor oil all over. Then they split. Next time it rained, it all came through, the rain, the oil. Ruined everything in my aunt's house.'

'No kiddin', Belane? You touch my god-damned heart with that one! Now, let's talk! You want the Sparrow or you want us to walk out of here?'

'You're gonna loan me 10 grand, huh? Which I ain't even going to get and you're going to charge me 15% a month interest? You got any other sweet deals for me? I mean, look at it this way: if you were me would you touch this god-damned deal?'

'Belane,' Sanderson smiled, 'one of the few things in the world that I am grateful for is that I am *not* you.'

Both of his monkeys smiled at that one.

'You sleep with these guys, Sanderson?'

'Sleep? What the hell you mean, sleep?'

'Sleep. Close your eyes. Play hand up the cheek. Stuff like that.'

'Belane, I ought to bust you up so you're less than a fart in an empty church!'

Both of his monkeys giggled at that one.

I inhaled, exhaled. Somehow, I felt as if I were going a bit mad. But I often felt that way.

'So, Sanderson, you say you can put the Sparrow in my hand?'

'Beyond a doubt.'

'Well, screw you.'

'What?'

'I said, "screw you!" '

'What's the matter with you, Belane? Going a bit mad?'

'Yeah. Yeah. That's it.'

'Just a moment . . .'

Sanderson gathered his two monkeys close to him. I could hear them buzzing and chirping. Then the huddle broke.

Sanderson looked solemn.

'It's your last shot, punk.'

'What? What is?'

'We've decided to let you have the bird for 5 grand.'

'3 grand.'

'4 grand is our final offer.'

'Where's the fucking papers?'

'I got 'em here . . .'

He reached into his coat and threw them on the desk. I tried to read them. There was much legal jargon. I was to sign for a loan from the Acme Executioners. 15% interest a month. I could make that out. Also, something else.

'This thing still reads as a 10 grand loan.'

'Oh, Mr. Belane, we can fix that,' said Sanderson. He snatched the papers, crossed out the 10, changed it to 4, initialed it. He flipped the papers back on my desk.

'Now, sign . . .'

I found a pen. Then I did it. I signed the god-damned thing.

Sanderson snatched the papers up and put them back in his coat.

'Thanks a bunch, Mr. Belane. Have a nice day.'

He and his two monkeys turned to leave.

'Hey, where's the Red Sparrow?'

Sanderson stopped, turned.

'Oh,' he said.

'Yeah, oh,' I said.

'Meet us at the Grand Central Market, tomorrow afternoon, 2 p.m.'

'That's a big place. Where?'

'Just find the butcher shop. Stand by the hogs' heads. We'll find you.'

'Hogs' heads?'

'Right. We'll find you.'

Then they turned and walked out of there. I sat there looking at the walls. I had a vague feeling that I had been screwed.

48

So, it was 2 p.m. I was at the Grand Central Market. I had found the butcher shop and I stood at the hogs' heads. The holes in the skulls, where the eyes had been, looked at me. I looked back, took a puff at my cigar. So many things to make a man sad. The poor boiled those skulls for soup.

I wondered if I had been set up. These guys might never show.

A poor soul walked toward me. He was dressed in rags. As he got close I spoke to him, 'Hey, buddy, you

got a dollar for a beer? My damned tongue is hanging
out . . .'

The miserable bastard turned and walked off. Sometimes I gave, sometimes I didn't. It all depended upon
how my feet hit the floor in the morning. Maybe. Who
knew?

Well, there wasn't enough money to go around.
There never had been. I didn't know what to do about
it.

Then I saw them. Sanderson and his two monkeys.
They were approaching me. Sanderson was smiling and
carrying something covered by a cloth. It looked like a
bird cage under there. Was it a bird cage?

Then they stood in front of me. Sanderson looked
over at the hogs' heads.

'Belane, just be glad you're not a hog's head.'

'Why?'

'Why? A hog's head can't fuck, eat candy, watch TV.'

'What you got under the rag, Sanderson?'

'Something for you, baby, you're going to like it.'

'Sure,' said one of the monkeys.

'Yep,' said the other.

'These guys ever disagree with you, Sanderson?'

'Uh-uh, that would be death.'

'We wanna live,' said one of them.

'To a ripe old age,' said the other.

'Like I said, Sanderson, what you got in the cage?'

'Oh, this ain't your cage, this cage is empty.'

'You gonna give me an empty cage?'

'This is the decoy, Belane.'

'What do you need a decoy for?'

'We just like to play. We're playful.'

'Great. Now, where's the real cage?'

'In the front seat of your car.'

'My car? How did you . . .'

'Oh, we're good at that, Belane.'

'But why did you say I was going to like it?'

'Like what?'

'That cage you're holding there. You said I was going to like it and your two doormats agreed.'

'Just playing. We like to play. It was small talk.'

'Small talk? When you going to stop playing? When is the talk going to get large?'

'The front seat of your car, Belane. Check it out. We're going now. See you around town. In 30 days.'

They walked off. And I was left with the hogs' heads.

Well. I got out of there and walked toward parking. As I walked along I saw a wino leaning against a wall, his head down. The flies were having at him. I stopped and stuck a dollar in his pocket.

Then I was into parking. I walked toward the car, got in. There was another bird cage there, covered. I made sure all the windows were shut. Then I took a deep breath and pulled the cloth away. There was a bird in there. A red one. I looked close. It wasn't a sparrow. It was a canary dyed red. Umm umm. Ow. Oh.

They could have gotten a sparrow and dyed it red. No, they had to get a fucking canary. And I couldn't turn it loose. It would starve out there. I had to keep it. I was stuck.

And taken.

I started the car and drove out of there. I hustled the signals and finally got on the freeway. As I drove along I heard a little sound. The cage door had popped open and the bird had gotten out. It began to fly wildly about the car. The red canary. A guy in the other lane saw the action and began laughing at me. I gave him the finger. A huge dark scowl crossed his face. I saw him reach. He rolled down his window and pointed the gun at me, fired. He was a lousy shot. He missed. But I felt the wind from the bullet passing by my nose. The bird flew wildly and I gunned the car. There was a bullet hole in each of my windows, one made going in, the other out. I didn't look back. I had it to the floor. I kept it there until I got to my exit. Then I looked back. My friend was nowhere in sight. I felt the bird then. He was standing on the top of my head. I could feel him there. Then he let go. I could feel the bird droppings as they dropped.

Not a very good day.

Not a hell of a very good day for me.

49

I was in the office. I think it was a Wednesday. There were no new cases. I was still on the Red Sparrow caper, mulling it over, sorting out my moves. The only move I could think of was moving out of town before 25 days were up.

No way. They weren't going to run my ass out of Hollywood. I *was* Hollywood, what was left of it.

There was a very polite knock on the door.

'Yeah,' I said, 'drag it in.'

The door opened and here was this little fellow, dressed all in black, black shoes, black suit, even a black shirt. Only his necktie was green. Lime green. His gorilla loomed up behind him. Only a gorilla had more brains.

'I'm Johnny Temple,' he said, 'and this is my assistant, Luke.'

'Luke, eh? Tell me, what does he do?'

'Whatever I tell him.'

'Why don't you tell him to leave?'

'What's the matter, Belane, don't you like Luke?'

'Do I have to?'

Luke took a step forward. His face began to contort, he looked as if he were going to cry.

'You not like me, Belane?' Luke asked.

'Luke, you stay out of this,' said Temple.

'Yeah, stay out of this,' I said.

'You like me, Johnny?' Luke asked.

'Of course, of course! Now, Luke, you go stand in front of the door and don't let anybody in or out.'

'You too?'

'What do you mean, Luke?'

'I not let you in or out either?'

'No, Luke, you let me in and out. But nobody else. Not until I tell you to.'

'OK.'

Luke walked over and stood in front of the door.

Temple pulled up a chair, sat down.

'I'm here from Acme Executioners. I'm here to brief you. Our salesman, Harold Sanderson . . .'

'Salesman? You call that guy a salesman?'

'One of our best.'

'I guess he is,' I admitted, 'look at that!'

I pointed to the bird cage hanging in the corner. Inside was the red canary.

'He sold me that,' I said.

'Harry could sell the skin off a dead body,' said Temple.

'He probably has,' I said.

'That's neither here nor there. We are here to brief you.'

'Go ahead but make it brief.'

'You're not funny, Belane. We loaned you 4 grand at 15% interest a month. That will be $600. We want to make sure you understand everything before we come to collect.'

'Suppose I don't have it?'

'We always collect, Mr. Belane, in one way or the other.'

'You break legs, Temple?'

'Our methods vary.'

'Suppose those methods fail. Would you have a man killed for 4 grand and interest?'

Temple pulled out a pack of smokes, tapped one out, lit it with his lighter. Then he slowly inhaled, exhaled.

'You bore me, Belane.'

Then he said, 'Luke . . .'

'Yes, Johnny?'

'See that red bird in the cage?'

'Yes, Johnny.'

'Luke, I want you to walk over there, take that bird out of that cage and I want you to eat it alive.'

'Yes, Johnny.'

Luke started to walk over to the cage.

'JESUS, TEMPLE, STOP HIM! STOP HIM! STOP HIM!' I yelled.

'Luke,' said Temple, 'I've changed my mind, I don't want you to eat that bird alive.'

'Should I roast him first, Johnny?'

'No, no, just leave him alone. Go back and stand by the door.'

'Yes, Johnny.'

Temple looked at me.

'You see, Belane, we always have to collect one way or the other. And if one method doesn't work we move to another. We have to stay in business. We are known all over town. Our reputation is acknowledged everywhere. We can allow nothing or no one to besmirch that reputation. I want you to understand this thoroughly.'

'I think I get it, Temple.'

'Fine. Your first due date comes up in 25 days. You have been briefed.'

Temple stood up, smiled.

'Good day,' he said.

He turned.

'All right, Luke, open the door, we are leaving.'

Luke did that. Temple turned and gave me a last look. He was no longer smiling. Then they were gone.

I walked over to the cage and looked at my red canary. Some of the dye was wearing off, some of the natural yellow was beginning to show through. It was a nice bird. It looked at me and I looked back. Then it made a little bird sound: 'cheep!' and somehow that made me feel good. I was easy to please. It was the rest of the world that was the problem.

50

I decided to go to my apartment and have a few drinks. I had to think it through. I was at a dead end with the Red Sparrow and with my life. I drove on over, parked it, got out. I had to get out of that apartment. I'd been there 5 years. It was like I was building a nest, only nothing was hatching. Too many people knew where I lived. I walked up to my door, unlocked it. I pushed it open, there was something in the way. A body. A babe stretched there. No, hell, it was one of those inflatable dolls, one of those inflatable things some guys made love to. Not me, though, buddy.

The babe was fully inflated. I picked her up and carried her to the couch. Then I noticed a sign around her throat: 'Belane, lay off the Red Sparrow or you'll be less than this dead rubber fuck.'

Nice note. So, I'd had a visitor. Somebody who didn't want me on the case. But it gave me hope. The Red Sparrow must truly exist or people wouldn't be acting like this. All I had to do was pick up the trail. There had to be one. There were too many scratchings going on. I could be on something big. Maybe international. Maybe something from another world? The Red Sparrow. Son of a bitch, matters were getting interesting. I made myself a nice drink, had a hit. Then the phone rang. I picked it up.

'Yeah?'

'Pooper, what are you doing?'

A chill ran up my back. It was one of my x-wives, Penny. Last I knew, 5 years or so ago, after our divorce, she had vanished off into somewhere with a guy who worked the tables at Vegas, a Sammy.

'Sorry, you have the wrong number, madam.'

'I know your voice, Pooper. How ya doin'?'

She had this nickname for me. Totally groundless.

'Doin' lousy,' I said.

'You need company.'

'Uh-uh.'

'You never knew what you needed, Pooper.'

'Maybe not but I know what I don't need.'

'I'm comin' up.'

'Uh-uh.'

'I'm downstairs, I'm phoning from the hall phone.'

'Where's Sammy?'

'Who?'

'Sammy.'

'Oh, that . . . Listen, I'm comin' up.'

Penny hung up. I felt awful, as if somebody had smeared shit all over me. I drained my drink and made another. Then there was the knock. I opened the door. There was Penny, 5 years older and 30 pounds heavier. She smiled an awful smile.

'Glad to see me?' she asked.

'Come on in,' I said. She followed me into the other room.

'Fix me a drink, Pooper!'

'Yeah . . .'

'Hey, what's that?'

'What?'

'That rubber thing. That rubber woman.'

'That's an inflatable doll.'

'You use it?'

'Not yet.'

'What's it doing here?'

'I don't know. Here's your drink.'

Penny pushed the doll to the floor and sat down with her drink. She took a hit.

'I've missed you, Pooper.'

'Missed what?'

'Oh, little things.'

'Like what?'

'Can't think of them now.'

She gulped her drink, looked over at me, smiled.

'I need some money, Pooper. Sammy skipped out with everything I had.'

'I'm in hock, Penny. Some guy's going to bust my sack if I don't pay the interest on a loan.'

I walked out and poured two more drinks, came back.

'Just a little money, Pooper.'

'I don't have it, for Christ's sake.'

'I'll give you some head. Remember, I used to give good head?'

'Look, all I've got is $20. Here . . .'

I dug it out and handed it to her.

'Thanks . . .'

Penny stuck it into her purse. We sat there, sipping at the drinks.

'We had some good times together,' she said.

'Early,' I said.

'I don't know,' she said, 'I started getting depressed.'

'Listen, we divorced because we couldn't make it.'

'Yeah,' she said. 'You don't fuck that thing, do you?'

'No, somebody left it here.'

'Who?'

'I don't know. Somebody's playing games with me.'

'You want some head?'

'No.'

'Can I stay here and drink a while?'

'How long?'

'A couple of hours.'

'All right.'

'Thanks, Pooper.'

When she left she was pretty drunk. I gave her another $20 for a cab. She said it wasn't far.

After she left I just sat there. Then I picked up the inflatable doll and sat it on the couch next to me. I had a vodka and tonic. It was a quiet evening. A quiet evening in hell. As the earth burned like a rotten log full of termites.

51

You have no idea how fast 25 days can go when you don't want them to go.

I was sitting in my office when the door pushed open. It was Johnny Temple. He had two new apes with him.

'Acme Executioners,' he said, 'we've come to collect.'

'I don't have it, Johnny.'

'You don't have the 600 bucks?'

'I don't have 60 bucks.'

Johnny sighed. 'We're gonna have to make an example of you.'

'Like what? You gonna rough me up for a lousy 600 bucks?'

'Not rough you up, Belane, but take you out. All the way.'

'I don't believe you.'

'Don't matter what you believe,' said one of the apes.

'Yeah, don't matter,' said the other ape.

'Now wait a minute, Johnny. You say you're gonna take me out for 600 bucks on a 4 grand loan? A loan I was suckered into and never saw? And you never delivered the Red Sparrow. How about the guys who owe you *big money*? Why don't you take them out? Why me?'

'Well, Belane, it's like this. We take you out for owing a pittance. The word gets out around town. And it really puts the *fear* into those who owe us big! Because they figure if we can do this to you over almost nothing, then they are going to know what the hell is going to happen to them. Get it?'

'Yeah,' I said, 'I get it. But we're talking about my life here, you know. It's like it doesn't matter, you know.'

'It doesn't,' said Johnny. 'We're running a business. Business has never been concerned with anything but profit.'

'I can't believe that this is happening,' I said, sliding the desk drawer open.

'Hold it!' said one of the apes, stepping forward and poking a luger in my ear. 'I'll take that piece!'

He slid my .32 out of there.

'You move fast for a fat fuck,' I told him.

'Yeah,' he smiled.

'All right, Belane,' said Johnny Temple, 'we're all going for a little ride.'

'But it's broad daylight!'

'All the better to see you with. Come on, get up!'

I got up from behind the desk and the two apes squeezed me between them. Temple walked behind us. We left the office and walked down to the elevator. I reached out and pressed the button myself.

'Thanks, punk,' said Johnny.

It came up. The doors opened. Empty. They shoved me on. Down we went. Empty feeling. First floor. Lobby. We walked out on the street. It was crowded. People walking everywhere. I thought, I'll scream out, hey, these guys are going to kill me! But I was afraid if I did that, they'd do it then. I walked along with them. It was a beautiful day. Then we were at their car. The two apes got in the back with me in the middle. Johnny Temple took the wheel up front. He pulled out into traffic.

'This whole thing is a bad senseless dream,' I said.

'It ain't no dream, Belane,' said Johnny Temple.

'Where you takin' me?'

'Griffith Park, Belane, we're going to have a little picnic. A little picnic on one of those isolated trails. Secluded. Private.'

'How can you fucking guys be so cold?' I asked.

'It's easy,' said Johnny, 'we were born that way.'

'Yeah,' laughed one of the apes.

We drove along. I still couldn't believe it was happening. Maybe it wouldn't happen. Maybe at the last moment they'd tell me it was all a joke. Just trying to teach me a lesson. Something like that.

Then we were there. Johnny parked the car.

'All right. Get him out boys. We're going for a little walk.'

One of the apes yanked me out of the side of the car. Then each ape had me by an arm. Johnny walked along behind us. Then we were on a discarded horse path. It was covered with brush and tree branches and the sun was blocked off.

'Listen you guys,' I said. 'This is enough. Tell me this whole thing is a joke and we'll all go have a drink somewhere.'

'It's no joke, Belane, we're taking you out. All the way,' said Johnny.

'600 dollars. I can't believe it. I can't believe the world works this way.'

'It does. We gave you our reasoning. Keep walking,' said Johnny.

We kept walking. Then Johnny said, 'This looks like a good spot. Turn around, Belane.'

I did. I saw the gun. Johnny fired. Four shots. Right in the gut. I fell on my face but managed to roll on my back.

'Thanks a bunch, Temple,' I managed to say.

They walked off.

I don't know. I must have passed out. Then I was

back. I knew I didn't have long. I was losing blood, lots of it.

Then I seemed to be hearing music, music like I'd never heard before. And then it happened. Something was taking shape, appearing before me. It was red, red, and like the music, a red I had never seen before. And there it was:

THE RED SPARROW.

Gigantic, glowing, beautiful. Never a sparrow so large, so real, never one so magnificent.

It stood before me. And then – there was Lady Death. Standing beside the Sparrow. And never had *she* looked so beautiful.

'Belane,' she said, 'you really got suckered into a bad play.'

'I can't talk much, Lady . . . Fill me in on the whole matter.'

'Your John Barton is a very perceptive man. He sensed that the Red Sparrow existed, was real, somehow, somewhere. And that you would find it. Now you have. Most of the others – Deja Fountain, Sanderson, Johnny Temple – were con artists, trying to trick and bleed you. Since you and Musso's are the last remnants of the old Hollywood, the real Hollywood, they got the idea you had big money.'

I smiled.

'Lady, how about that inflated doll in my room?'

'That? That was the mailman. He'd heard you were on the Red Sparrow caper and he wanted to pay you back one more time for the beating. He jimmied your door and left the thing there.'

'Now what, Lady?'

'I'm leaving you with the Red Sparrow. You're in good hands. Goodbye, Belane, it's been fun.'

'Yeah ...'

And there I was with that gigantic glowing bird. It stood there.

This can't be true, I thought. This isn't the way it is supposed to happen. No, this isn't the way it is supposed to happen.

Then, as I watched, the Sparrow slowly opened its beak. A huge void appeared. And within the beak was a vast yellow vortex, more dynamic than the sun, unbelievable.

This isn't the way it happens, I thought again.

The beak opened wide, the Sparrow's head moved closer and the blaze and the blare of yellow swept over and enveloped me.

CHARLES BUKOWSKI is one of America's best-known contemporary writers of poetry and prose, and, many would claim, its most influential and imitated poet. He was born in Andernach, Germany, to an American soldier father and a German mother in 1920, and brought to the United States at the age of three. He was raised in Los Angeles and lived there for fifty years. He published his first story in 1944 when he was twenty-four and began writing poetry at the age of thirty-five. He died in San Pedro, California, on March 9, 1994, at the age of seventy-three, shortly after completing his last novel, *Pulp* (1994).

During his lifetime he published more than forty-five books of poetry and prose, including the novels *Post Office* (1971), *Factotum* (1975), *Women* (1978), *Ham on Rye* (1982), and *Hollywood* (1989). Among his most recent books are the posthumous editions of *What Matters Most Is How Well You Walk Through the Fire* (1999), *Open All Night: New Poems* (2000), *Beerspit Night and Cursing: The Correspondence of Charles Bukowski and Sheri Martinelli, 1960–1967* (2001), and *The Night Torn Mad with Footsteps: New Poems* (2001).

All of his books have now been published in translation in over a dozen languages and his worldwide popularity remains undiminished.